UNHOLY SCANDAL

BASED ON A TRUE STORY

UNHOLY SCANDAL

BASED ON A TRUE STORY

Patti Hornstra

TEAM ELEVEN PUBLISHING
Gloucester, VA

Hornstra, Patti. Unholy Scandal.
Copyright © 2022 by Patti Hornstra

Published by Team Eleven Publishing:
www.teamelevenpublishing.com

Cover Design: Fresh Design
Editing: Kate Johnson Creative Services

Publisher's Cataloging-In-Publication Data
(Prepared by The Donohue Group, Inc.)

Names: Hornstra, Patti, author.
Title: Unholy scandal / Patti Hornstra.
Description: [Gloucester, Virginia] : Team Eleven Publishing, [2022] |
"Based on a True Story."
Identifiers: ISBN 9781736918104 (print) | ISBN 9781736918111 (ebook)
Subjects: LCSH: Catholic Church--Clergy--Sexual behavior--Fiction. | Child sexual
abuse--Fiction. | Catholic schools--Virginia--Fiction. | Boys' schools--Virginia--
Fiction. | Scandals--Fiction.
Classification: LCC PS3608.O76735 U54 2022 (print) |
LCC PS3608.O76735 (ebook) | DDC 813/.6--dc23

AUTHOR'S NOTES

This book is a fictionalized account of a true story and was written to honor the memory of a dear friend. While the main character is based on a real person, the story is not to be taken as a biographical account.

The characters and plot were developed to reflect the social/religious climate of the Catholic Church from the mid-1990s to the early 2000s. This was a time when the sex abuse crisis in the United States Catholic Church was rapidly unfolding, and this story was written in hopes of providing a balanced view of the impact of that crisis on a variety of levels. It is a *behind the scenes* account of one character's life as a Catholic priest who was accused of abuse.

The story is written in first person narrative form, which I believe is the most effective way for you, the reader, to connect with the main character and to understand his journey. That journey began in the early years of his life, when he began serving the Church as a young child, and ended after six decades when he was abandoned and ostracized by the very institution that he had loved and served for so many years.

I have made every effort to be factually accurate when it comes to the details about the Church (hierarchy, definitions, etc.) and the social/religious climate during the time this story takes place.

Unholy Scandal is the story of Father Paul Freemont, a priest accused of the sexual abuse of minors. It is divided into four parts.

Part One is the story of his life, from the time he became enraptured with the Catholic Church as a young child to the time he was accused of sexual abuse.

Part Two begins with the fallout from those accusations and the impact they had on his life's ministry as a priest.

Part Three chronicles the years of uncertainty that haunted him from the time he was removed from priestly ministry for the last time until his death.

Part Four contains information that may be helpful to non-Catholics (and some Catholics as well) as they try to understand the hierarchy and history of the Church, as well as the terminology used in telling Father Paul's story. Part Four is a supplement to the story and is very basic in its content. It may be helpful to refer to sections of Part Four (particularly the definitions and hierarchy) while reading Parts One, Two, and Three if terms are unfamiliar.

Because *Unholy Scandal* is written in the first person, as if Father Paul is telling his own story (and because it is *based* on a true story), it may be easy to forget that this book is a work of fiction.

I'm a firm believer that there are not two, but rather three, sides to every story; the truth can often be found somewhere in the middle of the opposing sides. I (the writer) offer no opinion as to the guilt or innocence of my fictional character, Father Paul Freemont; I am simply telling his story. To be more accurate, I am telling *his side* of the story.

This is obviously a sensitive topic, and I've made every effort to address it respectfully. My purpose for writing this is to provide enlightenment and (hopefully) a balanced perspective. I pray that all victims of abuse find peace and healing and that all those guilty of abuse are brought to justice.

PRAYER FOR HEALING VICTIMS OF ABUSE
~ USCCB

God of endless love, ever caring, ever strong, always present, always just: You gave your only Son to save us by the blood of his cross.

Gentle Jesus, shepherd of peace, join to your own suffering the pain of all who have been hurt in body, mind, and spirit by those who betrayed the trust placed in them.

Hear our cries as we agonize over the harm done to our brothers and sisters. Breathe wisdom into our prayers, soothe restless hearts with hope, steady shaken spirits with faith: Show us the way to justice and wholeness, enlightened by truth and enfolded in your mercy.

Holy Spirit, comforter of hearts, heal your people's wounds and transform our brokenness. Grant us courage and wisdom, humility and grace, so that we may act with justice and find peace in you.

We ask this through Christ, our Lord.

Amen.

PRAYER FOR PRIESTS

~ Pope Benedict XVI

2nd Annual Global Rosary Relay for Priests, July 1, 2011

Lord Jesus Christ, eternal High Priest, you offered yourself
to the Father on the altar of the cross and through the
outpouring of the Holy Spirit gave Your priestly people a
share in Your redeeming sacrifice.

Hear our prayer for the sanctification of our priests.
Grant that all who are ordained to the ministerial priesthood
may be ever more conformed to you, the Divine Master.

May they preach the Gospel with pure heart and clear conscience.
Let them be shepherds according to Your own heart,
single-minded in service to you and to the Church,
and shining examples of a holy, simple, and joyful life.

Through the prayers of the Blessed Virgin Mary, Your Mother
and ours, draw all priests and the flocks entrusted to their care
to the fullness of eternal life where you live and reign with
the Father and the Holy Spirit, one God, forever and ever.

Amen.

For Padre, who taught me that faith is the emptiness of not knowing and the fullness of not needing to know.

Yesterday is gone. Tomorrow has not yet come.
We have only today. Let us begin.

~ Mother Teresa

PREFACE

"Faith, the body of Christ," Father proclaimed as I approached,
my hands cupped together and outstretched toward him.

Again, I thought. He did it again.

A MESSAGE FROM LYNNE STRAHORN

There were plenty of Catholic churches to choose from in Fairview, Virginia in the 1990s; a surprising number, actually, for a southern state on the border of the Bible Belt, which tends to be dominated by evangelical Protestantism. Each Catholic church had its own distinct personality. There were conservative parishes and liberal ones, some in the inner-cities, others in the suburbs, some with Mass spoken entirely in Latin or Vietnamese and others with Mass in Spanish for the growing Hispanic population. Some people chose to attend the parish in their geographical district for the simple convenience of being close to home. Others were willing to drive a little farther, so they joined parishes based on emotional connection rather than geography, as my family had done. I attended a church that my family and I loved—and had no plans of leaving.

My plans changed when I met Father Paul Freemont and learned about the new church he planned to open in a nearby town on the outskirts of Fairview. The excitement of helping "found" a new parish was too much to resist for me and for some of my adventurous Catholic friends, so we jumped ship, left our home parishes, and went with Father Paul to become founding members of St. Edward Catholic Church in Springfield, Virginia, an upper-middle-class suburb just west of Fairview. We were nomadic Catholics. We rented space in the local middle school for Sunday liturgy and at a local Protestant church for liturgy on Saturday evenings. The weekly necessities were stored in our houses or in the trunks of our cars: candles, altar cloths, communion cups and plates, toys for the nursery. We were *church* like I'd never seen before and realize now that I will never see again. Camelot is the word that I've heard so many of my fellow founding Edwardians (that's what we called ourselves, the parishioners of St. Edward) use to describe it. St. Edward was our happiness, our peace, our haven.

Father Paul was the overwhelming draw that brought us to St. Edward. One meeting with him and you knew that you needed to be part of whatever it was that he was involved with. His excitement and enthusiasm sucked you in, made you want to be a part of this village, this family. He was quick to recognize others' talents. One minute you were talking to him after Mass, the next minute you were in charge of a new ministry or of some enormous new project that he had dreamed up. Father Paul had the uncanny ability to put just the right person in charge of just the right project. He selected, he delegated, and he stood back and watched us thrive. He loved us, we loved him, and we all loved St. Edward.

I was an "A-player" back then; we were the ones who headed ministries, served on the parish council, had our hands in everything. Life, for so many of us, revolved around St. Edward. We couldn't get enough of our priest or of our church.

I have many memories of Father Paul, but one of my favorites is of my first time carrying the cross as we processed in for Mass.

"Okay, now, walk slow and hold it high like an Episcopal," he instructed me as he snatched me from the pew and handed me a six-foot-tall, thirty-pound, top-heavy crucifix five minutes before nine o'clock Mass started. Carrying the cross was a big deal for me, an introverted Catholic convert who didn't like to stand out.

I had no interest in playing the role of crucifer that morning at St. Edward. But suddenly there I was, doing just that. This was a first for me, and it absolutely terrified me. Still, I walked slowly and held it high that day and many more Sundays after that, each time wondering how I got pulled into doing it again. But that's how it worked. We Edwardians wanted to please Father Paul. If a Catholic priest can be described as bewitching, then Father Paul Freemont was just that. And I, like so many other parishioners at St. Edward, was bewitched by him. Father Paul was dynamic, charismatic, theatrical, a rock-star of a priest. He was striking, but not necessarily in a handsome way. Maybe it was the thick, jet-black hair in a bowl-cut style (Ringo Starr in his younger days, minus the sideburns). He was not too tall, not too short, not too thin, not too large. He was average in his appearance, but that's where *average* stopped.

Somehow, he stood out in every social situation. He commanded the room, as if he were holding court. Maybe it was because he always looked completely put together, even in a polo shirt, jeans, and loafers with just the slightest hint of musk, his cologne of choice. Maybe it was the way he guarded himself socially, constantly turning the gold signet ring (worn on the ring finger of his left hand) as he spoke, that being the only giveaway that he was always slightly uncomfortable in social settings. Or maybe it was just the way he made you feel—as if you were the most important being in his life at that moment. Striking comes in many forms, doesn't it?

Father Paul was a gifted speaker. He captivated the congregation, his audience, when he preached, which was often to standing room only crowds. He was rarely still, preferring to walk while he spoke to the congregation, never needing notes to remind him of his message. The worship space at St. Edward was circular, in the round, which allowed him the freedom to stroll among the people as he preached. His homilies (sermons) left you wanting to hear more, whether or not you agreed with him. His liberal, progressive views were a breath of fresh air to some and an annoyance to others.

We wore nametags at St. Edward. We even had a special ministry whose job it was to order and distribute nametags for registered parishioners. Most parishioners had blue nametags, but the "A-players" had burgundy ones with the name of our ministry position engraved in white under our own name. Father always tried to call us by name as we received communion. He said that it made the sacrament more personal, hence the nametags. Every Sunday morning for months, he called me *Faith* as I received communion, that mysterious Catholic sacrament that made me truly one with Christ. There was one problem with that—my name is *Lynne*, not *Faith*. My nametag read *"Lynne Strahorn, Parish Council,"* yet he couldn't seem to get it right.

He did it again, I thought. Every Sunday morning for months. I finally asked Father Paul how he could make this same mistake repeatedly every week, nametag and all. His only explanation was that, yes, he knew my name was *Lynne,* but somehow, when he looked at me, the name *Faith* always came out of his mouth. We laughed many times about the mystery behind that, and we joked about what an aura of faith I must carry to cause him to lapse every time I walked up to him in the communion line. How ironic that it would be the events of his life that would test my faith more deeply than I ever imagined.

Starting new parishes was his genuine gift, and faithful Catholics left their home parishes in droves to follow him when he started a new one. He started a number of new parishes during his forty-plus years as a parish priest. St. Edward was his last. At first there were a few dozen of us who left our home parishes to help him start St. Edward. Within a few months, that number had grown to eight hundred, and thousands more joined during the fourteen years that he led the flock. The number of registered parishioners had surpassed seven thousand just a few years after he left the parish. By that time, he had become a controversial memory.

What follows is his story, told here in his words as it was told to me. It's a story of tragedy, of devastation, of humiliation, of one life ruined and of countless others changed forever.

INTRODUCTION

NOLO CONTENDERE

*In 1963, Henry Alford was indicted by the state of North Carolina on charges of first-degree murder, which could have resulted in the death penalty had he been convicted. He decided to plead guilty to a lesser charge of second-degree murder in order to avoid the death penalty. He appealed his conviction under the grounds that he was **forced** to plead guilty to the lesser charge to avoid being put to death. Thus, the Alford Plea: the defendant maintains innocence while admitting that there is sufficient evidence that a prosecutor could use to convince a judge and/or jury of guilt beyond a reasonable doubt. It is sometimes called a plea of* **no contest** *or* **nolo contendere***.*

The size of the crowd was daunting, filling the red brick steps of the Rutherford County courthouse and overflowing onto the sidewalk, the grass, the parking lot.

Even through the Xanax fog that clouded my thoughts and *almost* numbed the pain, I recognized the familiar chants.

"Our Father Who Art in Heaven . . ."

"Hail Mary, Full of Grace . . ."

"Glory Be to the Father. . ."

Hundreds of my most faithful followers, their faces a blur to me, were gathered there in the December chill, praying the Rosary, the quintessential Catholic prayer.

My attorney, Bob James, and I had planned carefully for that day.

"Don't wear the collar," Bob warned. He wanted to be certain that the small-town judge saw me as a normal guy rather than as the arrogant, above-the-law cleric presented by the media over the past few months. As if that were even possible: for me to be seen as normal. The media had portrayed me as a sexual predator, a monster, and there was nothing I could do to change that. If the judge had read any of the newspaper articles about me, and I was sure he had, then there was no way that he would see me as a normal guy.

I passed through the crowd feeling almost anonymous in my street clothes, missing the comfort of the black shirt and white collar that I had worn as a priest for almost forty years. The black-and-white clerical garb had once commanded respect. Lately, it had become a symbol of suspicion, and I wondered what people thought of me when I wore it outside of the parish walls. It occurred to me then that it no longer mattered what I wore, or what the judge thought of me. I had stood in that same courtroom just three months earlier and made my plea. Today was nothing more than a formality, the sentencing phase of this nasty legal trauma that had consumed my life, and the lives of so many St. Edward parishioners, for far too long. The judge had already made his decision. I had a pretty good idea of what that decision would be, but there were no guarantees. With any luck, I would be spared jail time; Bob felt certain that I would be released after sentencing. It almost didn't matter anymore; it just needed to end.

Three months ago, I made the decision to do whatever it took to bring this to a close and try to somehow rebuild my life. The judge had asked me two questions that day.

"Reverend Freemont, are you guilty of the three counts of felony assault that you have been charged with?"

"No, Your Honor, I am not guilty."

"Reverend Freemont, are you guilty of the two counts of misdemeanor assault that you have been charged with?"

"Your Honor, I'd like to plead *no contest* to those charges." All I could think of was that, finally, this might end. Bob had assured me that this plea was my best chance of staying out of jail and ending the media frenzy that had been my life for much of the past two years.

I had prayed about this plea, had lost way too much sleep over it, and had finally decided that Bob was right. An Alford Plea was the best way to end this nightmare. Bishop Robertson (my boss) had agreed with that decision. Like me, he just wanted this to be over.

"Your Honor, my client has decided to enter an Alford Plea," Bob added. "He is maintaining his innocence, but recognizes that some of the evidence presented in this case . . ."

I didn't hear anything after that, my head spinning with unrecognizable sounds rather than words. It was done; it was real. Soon, it would be over.

Now, three months later, I walked up those brick steps again. In just moments, I would hear the judge proclaim my fate, one man's decision about how I would spend the rest of my life. Bob and I took our seats in the courtroom, my two brothers and their families sitting in the row directly behind us. It suddenly felt like a television courtroom drama; the formality of the bailiff announcing the judge as he walked in, followed by the *all rise.*

The judge spoke for what seemed like an eternity, then he finally made his way to what I had been waiting to hear.

"Reverend Freemont," began the judge, "in light of the fact that you entered an Alford Plea in September, I have no choice but to sentence you according to the state guidelines associated with that plea. Therefore, I am sentencing you to a two-year jail term on each of the two counts of misdemeanor assault, with the two terms to run concurrently. I hereby suspend the entire two years, meaning that you will serve no jail time. I am also ordering that you remain on probation for the remainder of your life."

It was over. There were hugs, pats on the back, congratulations. I just wanted to leave, to run. I needed to get back to my parish and try to pretend that this had never happened.

PART ONE

THE BEGINNING

In the beginning was the Word: The Word
was with God and the Word was God.

He was with God in the beginning.

Through him all things came into being, not one thing
came into being except through Him.

What has come into being in Him was life,
life that was the light of men;

and light shines in darkness, and darkness
could not overpower it.

~ JOHN 1:1-5

CHAPTER ONE

CATHOLIC GHETTO

Then people brought little children to him, for him to lay his hands
on them and pray. The disciples scolded them,

but Jesus said, 'Let the little children alone, and do not stop them
from coming to me; for it is to such as these that the kingdom
of Heaven belongs.'

Then he laid his hands on them and went on his way.

~ MATTHEW 19:13-15

None of this makes sense unless you understand the background.
My entire world revolved around being Catholic. I grew up in a lower
middle-class neighborhood in the city of Fairview, Virginia. My neighborhood was called a Catholic Ghetto, a term used lovingly to describe
the way we lived. My neighbors were almost all Catholic, and as kids
we rode our bikes to our Catholic school, which was right next door to

the Cathedral, the Catholic church that was the center of our diocese and the home of our bishop. It was the type of neighborhood where you would leave for school in the morning, and your classmates would join you along the way. By the time you got to school, there were thirty-five or forty kids riding together. There were two Catholic schools—a grade school and a high school. Each grade level had no more than twenty or twenty-five students, so each school had about a hundred students total. An order of nuns, the Sisters of Mercy, taught our classes.

I made my First Communion when I was seven years old. Father Thomas, a priest assigned to the Cathedral, worked with the Sisters to prepare our first-grade class for our First Holy Communion. I had never met a priest in person until then. Until that point in my life, the priest had been a rigid figure on the altar, stiff and unapproachable. Father Thomas was so different, so human, that by the second time he taught our class, I knew I would be a priest when I grew up. I was completely spellbound; I wanted nothing more than to be a Father Thomas.

That's when my journey to the priesthood began, when I was seven years old. A week after my First Communion, I was leaving home on my bike at six-fifteen every morning to serve as an altar boy at seven o'clock daily Mass.

Almost every person I knew when I was growing up was Catholic. In my world, you were either a Catholic or a Protestant. In fact, I had exactly one Protestant friend, Arlene Dunn. Arlene and her family lived two doors down from me, and she was a Baptist, one of the more conservative Protestant denominations. I always wondered how her family ended up in the Catholic Ghetto. One afternoon when we were in the fifth grade, Arlene and I were walking around the neighborhood, and we walked past the Cathedral. I asked her if she wanted to see my church, and she asked if we were allowed to go inside and look around, as if we were about to enter a forbidden land. A Catholic cathedral must have been a very mysterious place for a ten-year-old Baptist girl in the 1950s.

I remember taking her inside to see the high ceilings, the ornately carved wood, the gold accents, the enormous statues, and the stained-glass windows. There were no lights on that day, just the colored sunlight streaming through the stained glass. I remember the smell, that distinct smell of an old church. Musty wood, incense, long extinguished candles. It was truly majestic, and I was bursting with pride because I felt certain that she'd never seen anything like it before, and *I* was the one who got to show it to her.

We walked down the center aisle, and when we were about halfway down, I stopped so that we could take a seat in one of the ancient, uncomfortable wooden pews. Before we stepped in to sit down, I showed her how to genuflect, which I'm sure was a sight to see. I must have looked quite serious as I went down on one knee, making the sign of the cross before I rose again to lead her in to take a seat. I pulled down a kneeler to show her how we prayed as Catholics. Kneeling down, I closed my eyes and kept my head bowed an extra-long time so that she would think I was very pious.

When we stood up, I walked her around the church, whispering, showing off as if it belonged to me alone. Arlene noticed a table holding a beautiful, large bronze box off to the side near the front of the church, which looked almost like a miniature altar. She asked me what the box was and why there was a candle blinking in front of the door of the box. I explained to her that the box was the tabernacle, and that Jesus was in the tabernacle. She looked a little confused by that, and I remember her asking, "Jesus *is in* the tabernacle?" I assured her that Jesus was really and truly *in* that tabernacle. By that point, she looked completely bewildered, and she wanted to know why she couldn't have Jesus in a tabernacle in her church. I made it clear to her that we Catholics were the *one, true Church*, quoted straight out of the catechism—Father Thomas and the Sisters of Mercy had taught me well in first grade!

I was an altar boy for almost twelve years, from the time I was seven years old until I graduated from high school. When I was in the ninth grade, my friend Percy Johns and I were selected to be the bishop's altar servers at daily Mass, which was a huge honor back then. The altar had to be ready by seven-fifteen every morning, because the bishop could show up anywhere between seven-fifteen and eight-fifteen. Sometimes the bishop showed up on time, sometimes he was late, and sometimes he didn't show up at all. If he wasn't there by eight-fifteen, then we knew he wasn't coming. We'd blow out the candles, fold everything up that we had placed on the altar, then we'd go to Percy's house for breakfast. We'd also be late for school. That was okay, being late, because we were technically serving the bishop. This would never happen like that today, but that was the world in the 1950s.

When you grew up in the Catholic Ghetto in the 1950s, there weren't a lot of options after high school graduation. Only about a third of my graduating class went to college. Most of the others went to work at places like the phone company (the girls), or the highway department (the boys).

Although I'd wanted to be a priest since the first grade, by the time I got to high school, I was a little torn about what I truly wanted to do with the rest of my life. Part of me wanted to go to a traditional college and study theater, while the other part wanted to go into the seminary to become a priest. But I'd also found a new passion: photography.

Throughout high school, I took photos for the school yearbook, for First Communion Masses, those types of things. I had learned photography from my father; he was self-taught and was actually very good. My father was a taxi driver when I was a young child, and he became a city bus driver when I was about twelve years old. He worked his way up and became a claims adjuster for the city transit system. Eventually, he was promoted to claims manager for the transit system. That's when he realized that his claims would be so much more accurate (and easier to process) if he could photograph accidents on-site and develop his own photos, so he learned photography.

Film development in the 1950s took time, at least a few days, so waiting for photographs to come back from the photo lab held up the claims process quite a bit. My father convinced his superiors at the transit system to invest in photo processing equipment to help speed things up. He took all of this very seriously; we weren't allowed to call it a dark room—we had to call it his photo lab.

The entire process fascinated me, much more so than my older brothers. They had no interest in photography. So, I tagged along with my father whenever I could, and he taught me what he knew about taking photos and processing them. I actually became a pretty good photographer myself, and he started letting me take some of the photos for the claims.

When I was seventeen years old, a priest from St. Bartholomew College came to visit my high school on a recruitment mission. St. Bartholomew not only had a seminary, but they also offered a degree in photography. Even better, they offered a full two-year photography scholarship. I applied for the scholarship, and I got it!

I made my decision, no studying theater. I was going into the seminary on a photography scholarship from St. Bartholomew. This was the hand of God—the best of both worlds. The college had a few sports programs, so I took those photos. I also took photos for the school newspaper and the yearbook. Father Anthony was in charge of the printed publications at St. Bartholomew, and he was an amazing photographer. I learned so much from him about portraits, bounce lighting, all kinds of things.

The first two years at St. Bartholomew were fairly routine: daily Mass, breakfast, class, homework. Classes were selected for you and consisted of the basics: the first two years of a language, Psych 101, two years each of English, math, and history. My whole life revolved around the Catholic Church, and I loved every minute of it. We went to daily Mass at six-thirty in the morning, so we were up early. Breakfast was at seven o'clock, classes started at seven-fifty sharp. The daily schedule would seem very strict by today's standards, but back then we didn't think it was strict at all.

Seminary classes started in my junior year, and although we still didn't get to choose the classes we took, we could declare a major because we were at that point officially seminarians. Of course, as seminary students, you had one choice for a major, and that was philosophy. The choice really wasn't a choice at all. I wasn't a particularly good student when it came to philosophy, but I made it through.

Becoming a Catholic priest is typically an eight-year process. The first four years are spent getting an undergraduate degree, often in philosophy, then another four years (sometimes five) taking graduate courses in theology. Some seminarians spend the entire time at the same college, but sometimes the bishop chooses to send the brightest of the seminary students to a different college for the graduate courses in the last four or five years of seminary.

I was certain that I'd get a letter during my senior year of undergraduate telling me that I was being transferred; I thought I was very bright! Well, the letter never came, so I stayed at St. Bartholomew. I spent seven of my eight college years at St. Bartholomew before the school ran out of money and shut down; money problems seem to plague Catholic colleges. Next, I transferred to St. Michael College where I finished my graduate degree and finally began my life as a Catholic priest.

CHAPTER TWO

CLASS OF 1965

My child, do not forget my teaching,
let your heart keep my principles,

since they will increase your length of days,
your years of life and your well-being.

Let faithful love and constancy never leave you:
tie them round your neck,

write them on the tablet of your heart.

Thus you will find favour and success in the sight of God
and of people.

Trust wholeheartedly in Yahweh, put no faith in your own perception;

acknowledge him in every course you take,
and he will see that your paths are smooth.

~ Proverbs 3:1-6

*With praise and thanksgiving to
Almighty God,
the Diocese of Fairview
joyfully announces and invites you to
the Ordination to the Holy Priesthood*

of

REVEREND MR. PHILLIP S. DAVID

REVEREND MR. PAUL E. FREEMONT

REVEREND MR. BENJAMIN P. GALLAGHER

REVEREND MR. SHELTON M. MILLER

REVEREND MR. J. FORREST MURPHY

REVEREND MR. MARCUS B. REILLY

*through the invocation of the Holy Spirit
and the imposition of hand by His Excellency*

The Reverend Most Theodore P. Saunders

SATURDAY, THE FIFTEENTH OF MAY
NINETEEN HUNDRED AND SIXTY-FIVE
AT TEN O'CLOCK IN THE MORNING

CATHEDRAL OF THE HOLY CROSS
17 CATHEDRAL BOULEVARD
FAIRVIEW, VIRGINIA

My adult life began in 1965, the year I was ordained into the priesthood. It might sound silly to say now, but my ordination was truly mystical. It seemed like the entire world, or at least *my* entire world, came to the Cathedral to celebrate. There were so many people from St. Michael Seminary who came. I must have had thirty or forty out-of-town guests, plus my friends and family who lived in Fairview. I can remember this as if it were yesterday, and every time I pass the Cathedral it gets to me, even now.

The ceremony itself, the Rite of Ordination, was magical. It began with the long, slow procession down the center aisle of the Cathedral. The air was filled with what we seminarians had called the *smells and bells* of the Catholic Church—the woody smell of incense, symbolizing ascension and transcendence, as well as the faint chiming of the bells to signal the consecration of the precious Body and Blood of Christ.

During the ordination ceremony, Bishop Saunders put his hands on my head and prayed. He then put chrism oil all over my hands and wrapped them up in a long white cloth called a *manutergium*. The purpose of the cloth was to keep the oil from dripping onto my vestments or onto the floor. My manutergium was handmade for me by a special family friend, Sister Bernice. An intricate gold cross was beautifully embroidered on each end.

After the ceremony, they gave the cloth to my mother. She was supposed to pack it away in a special place so that when she died, her hands could be wrapped in it. The purpose was to remind people who came to her funeral visitation that she had a son who was a priest, since that was always seen as a special honor. When my mother died years later, we searched the house for the manutergium, but we never found it. I always wondered what happened to it.

My parents had a big party at their house after the ordination ceremony, and the last people stayed until just before midnight. Since I was out of cigarettes (practically everyone smoked back then), I walked to the all-night convenience store a few blocks away. I remember standing next to First Baptist Church, waiting for the green light to turn red so I could cross the street to get to the store, and it hit me full force—I was a priest!

I jumped around all over the place like a fool. There was a nice-looking stone fence that goes around that church, and I jumped up onto that stone fence and ran the length of it. Then I hopped all over the church steps. If anyone had been watching, they'd have thought that I had gone mad. I was just oozing and glowing; I was so happy, I literally couldn't contain myself.

There were six of us who were ordained together that day. We had all started together at St. Bartholomew seminary program in our junior year and had all been transferred together to St. Michael; we'd been together for six years. The bond we shared is impossible to explain. Your seminary brothers know you like no one else in the world. Not to say that we were all best friends, that's hardly the truth. We just probably knew each other as deeply as you can know another person. It took me years, perhaps decades, to realize how deeply they had each affected me in their own ways.

Shelton was my roommate the entire time. He was the devout one. If he wasn't in his room or in class, you were guaranteed to find him in the chapel. If he couldn't sleep at night, he'd get up and go to the chapel. He was very uneasy around women. That's one thing I'll always remember about him.

I lost touch with Shelton not too long after we were ordained. A few years after ordination, he had left the priesthood, which shocked me. I thought, if anyone was going to make it as a priest, it would have been Shelton; he was in the chapel all the time. I found out later that he had come out of the closet when he left the priesthood; you could have knocked me over with a feather. I lived with him in the same room for six years and never had any hint that he was gay. I always thought he was just uncomfortable with women. He died of AIDS (in the 1970s, long before AIDS became an epidemic). I didn't find out about all of this until months after he died. His mother sent me a letter to let me know what had happened.

Benjamin was the tight ass, an extreme rule follower. He took everything way too seriously. We had been ordained as deacons when we were in the seminary, a step on the path to being ordained as priests. One day, Benjamin declared himself to be *senior deacon*. I have no idea where he came up with that. If we were staying up past curfew or if he saw us drinking liquor, he'd tell us to stop immediately. I wasn't sure what he planned to do about it if we didn't do what he said, and so we just ignored him.

Benjamin was voted 'Most Likely to Become a Bishop.' He was definitely put on the fast track by the powers-that-be in the diocese. The bishop even sent him to school to get a Ph.D. in theology. Ironically, he ended up leaving the priesthood to marry an older woman, actually a nun, whom he met at church.

The good-looking one was Forrest; he was a clothes horse. He had more clothes than all the rest of us put together. We used to joke that Forrest never left his room until he had changed his outfit at least three times. Every time we went out, we had to wait for him. He wasn't a brilliant student, but he managed to graduate.

Forrest was the most easygoing of all of us; you could tell him anything. He loved the beach, anything to do with water, so he begged the bishop to assign him to a parish on the coast. The bishop finally agreed after a couple of years, and last I heard, Forrest was still working as a pastor at a church near the water in the eastern part of the state.

Phillip was the cocky one. He always acted as if he had no time for the rest of us, like he was too busy to be bothered. Phillip never fit in with us. He was very critical of everything, and he was over-the-top liberal. Phillip ended up joining me as a teacher at St. Joseph Seminary several years after our ordination; he taught a lot of the religion classes there.

He fell in love with a teacher, a nun, at the local Catholic girls' school, and he left the priesthood so they could get married. I heard that he got a great job working for a huge corporation, and he and his wife had four or five children.

Mark was the quiet one. He and I spent a lot of time together. Mark was truly just a nice guy. He was assigned to a parish in Portsmouth right after we were ordained, but he was only there for a year. After that, the bishop sent him to a parish in the northern part of the state. At that time, the diocese of Fairview was in the process of being split into two; Mark's parish was above the dividing line, so it ended up in the new northern diocese.

About four or five years after Mark was sent north, the bishop received a phone call from a young man who had attended Mark's parish in Portsmouth. He accused Mark of molesting him when he was a teenager. One afternoon, a few days after that phone call, Mark got in his car and went to a gun shop, bought a rifle, and went to a monastery an hour or so away. He said he was going to make a retreat. They found his body two days later along a path in the woods where he had shot himself.

And then there was me, the sixth member of the Class of 1965, so much like the others and so different at the same time. I like to think that I shared Shelton's level of devotion, although you wouldn't find me in the chapel if I went missing. Unlike Benjamin, I wasn't a rule follower. I would have rather asked forgiveness than permission. And no one ever would have expected me to be appointed a bishop. I learned the importance of appearance from Forrest, and I've carried that with me since seminary. Phillip and I shared liberal views, both socially and politically, but our similarities stopped there. In fact, his arrogant attitude often offended me. I tried to emulate Mark more than any of the others. His genuine kindness made me strive to be a better person.

I've often wondered what the other five of my classmates called me behind my back. The progressive one? The liberal one?

The naïve one, perhaps?

CHAPTER THREE

EARLY ASSIGNMENTS

My child, if you aspire to serve the Lord,
prepare yourself for an ordeal.

Be sincere of heart, be steadfast,
and do not be alarmed when disaster comes.

Cling to him and do not leave him,
so that you may be honoured at the end of your days.

Whatever happens to you, accept it, and in the uncertainties
of your humble state, be patient,

since gold is tested in the fire, and the chosen
in the furnace of humiliation.

Trust him and he will uphold you,
follow a straight path and hope in him.

~ Sirach 2:1-6

My first assignment as a priest was to St. Mark Catholic Church in Alexandria, an old, gothic church located about a hundred miles from my hometown. I was associate pastor there, so my job was to assist the pastor. There were four priests, me included, living in a huge three-story rectory, which was designed for four priests to live there full-time. It also had a couple of guest rooms, plus a special guest room that was reserved for the bishop to use when he came to town. When the bishop came to Alexandria, he always stayed at St. Mark because it looked like a five-star hotel.

I drove to St. Mark in a beautiful, brand-new, white Pontiac Bonneville that my parents had bought me as an ordination gift. They had scrimped and saved all their lives to buy my brothers and me each a new car for college graduation. I had two suitcases in the trunk of my car, nothing else. I walked through the back door into the kitchen and met the caretaker, a wonderful woman named Barbara. She had the darkest skin I'd ever seen, and she was as round as she was tall. She was a fabulous cook; the smells coming out of that kitchen were heavenly. I got the biggest hug, the biggest welcome from her, as if she'd known me all my life.

"Let me call Father, he'll be so happy that you're here." She went to the intercom and buzzed the pastor's suite of rooms. Father George Banks came downstairs after about ten minutes and walked into the room with a look on his face that let me know my arrival was a great inconvenience.

The first thing he said to me was, "Call me Father, do not call me by my first name." Then he looked at his watch. It was three-thirty in the afternoon. He said, "You have to hear confessions at four o'clock. Barbara will show you to your room." And he disappeared. Welcome to the priesthood, I thought.

My duties as associate pastor filled my weekends, and I stayed busy during the week. I enrolled in a graduate program at St. Agnes University in downtown Alexandria for my master's degree in secondary education. I also worked two jobs while I was assigned to St. Mark. Most of my classes were in the late afternoon or evening, and my weekdays were split between teaching religious education classes at the Catholic high school a few mornings a week and working as the Director of the Board of Catholic Services the rest of the time.

The mission of Catholic Services was to assist people who needed help with housing, medical and legal issues, that sort of thing, but primarily it served as an adoption agency. Sometimes the paths of my work at the high school and my work at Catholic Services crossed. There's one crossing in particular that I'll never forget. I was presiding at Mass one Sunday morning when I saw two familiar couples in line for communion. One couple I had met at Catholic Services when they came in and asked for my help. They were childless and had been desperate to adopt a baby. That day in the communion line, the mother carried an infant girl in her arms while the father beamed with pride. The couple standing in line directly behind them were high school sweethearts, and I had been their religion teacher. I had also counseled them (and their parents) through a teenage pregnancy and the hard decision to place their baby girl up for adoption. Neither couple had any idea of their connection to each other that day in the communion line, but witnessing those two couples standing together, their bond unknown to each other, was one of the most special moments in my entire career.

When I wasn't in class, I spent my evenings meeting with couples who wanted to be married in the Church or with non-Catholics who wanted to join the Catholic Church. There wasn't a lot of free time, but it was a wonderful period in my life. This was during the mid to late 1960s, and the church had been going through a lot of changes since Vatican II (when the Church made a move to adapt to the modern world). Until this point, Mass had been in Latin, including the hymns. St. Mark had no hymn books at all since few, if any, parishioners spoke Latin.

I decided to put together some English hymn books with help from a group of parishioners with whom I had become friends; we actually printed them on the copier and stapled them together. We were all eager for the Church to move in a more modern direction, and we could see it slowly beginning to happen. Even though something as simple as stapling together English language hymn books was seen as ultra-progressive at the time, Father Banks tolerated it. As conservative as he was, he knew that the direction of the Catholic Church as a whole was changing whether or not he wanted it to.

There were changes going on in our diocese as well. Theodore Saunders, the bishop who ordained me, was our bishop then. He was assigned to the Cathedral in Fairview, but the diocese at that time still included the entire state of Virginia, so he was in charge of a pretty sizeable area. Bishop Saunders had two goals. One, he wanted to build a Catholic hospital in Fairview. Two, he wanted to build a high school seminary, all boys, of course, somewhere in the diocese. Those were two pretty enormous projects to take on at the same time, but Saunders was determined to accomplish both and leave them as his legacy. There were meetings all over the diocese, the entire state, to raise funds for the hospital and the seminary. They set teams up to go to every Catholic household in the state and ask each family for a pledge. My dad and his best friend, Lee, were a team. They worked in the central part of Fairview. Every Sunday afternoon for months, they visited Catholic families and got pledges. There were teams all over the state doing the same thing, and quite a bit of money was raised.

Bishop Saunders accomplished both of his goals. The hospital took much longer to build, obviously. St. Elizabeth's Hospital opened its doors in 1966, a year after I was ordained. The seminary had already opened five years before I was ordained.

At first, the seminary seemed to flourish. Enrollment was high in the early years, and many of the graduates went on to become priests. But things at the seminary began to change as the Catholic Church became more progressive. Eventually, the seminary was struggling to maintain enrollment, and Bishop Saunders decided that it was time for a new staff and administration to take over.

Three years after I arrived at St. Mark in Alexandria, the bishop sent me to Rutherford County, about twenty miles west of my hometown of Fairview, to be part of the new staff that he hoped would save the struggling seminary.

I've often wondered what my life would have been like if that had never happened.

CHAPTER FOUR

ST. JOSEPH SEMINARY

Only a few of you, my brothers, should be teachers, bearing
in mind that we shall receive a stricter judgement.

For we all trip up in many ways. Someone who does not
trip up in speech has reached perfection and is able
to keep the whole body on a tight rein.

Once we put a bit in the horse's mouth, to make it do what we want,
we have the whole animal under our control.

Or think of ships: no matter how big they are,
even if a gale is driving them, they are directed by a tiny
rudder wherever the whim of the helmsman decides.

~ JAMES 3:1-4

In 1960, five years before I was ordained, St. Joseph Seminary, an all-male high school, opened its doors with a director, five priests (who were the teachers), and sixty-five students. The director was Father Frank Celeste. Everyone who knew him said that Father Frank was either a saint or a fool to take on that job. It was hard, thankless work, but he did a great job of getting the five priests (the teachers—none of whom had any teaching experience), certified and endorsed to teach their respective subjects. They taught the basics that you'd find at any high school—math, English, history, science—and they also taught religion. The school attracted very bright kids, boys, who were interested in going into the priesthood. It also attracted some kids who liked the idea of leaving home and experiencing the adventure of going to boarding school.

High school seminaries were rigid at that time, but Father Frank had a different concept of what a seminary should be like. He relaxed the dress code to try to make the kids more comfortable. Frank played hymns on the loudspeaker in the morning to wake them up, instead of ringing bells in the halls. Back then, that was considered being extremely progressive, almost radical. This was during the time when the Church was still very conservative; Mass was in Latin, hymns were in Latin.

Playing hymns as a wake-up call still sounds conservative, but it was much more liberal than ringing bells in the halls. The school opened just two years before Vatican II, a time of sweeping change in the Catholic Church. The entire world seemed to be unraveling then. News stories were all about the Vietnam War, protests, and the civil rights movement. Tie-dyed T-shirts, headbands, and peace signs were everywhere you looked.

Father Frank was liberal, and he saw that the Church was becoming more liberal and progressive as the world changed. He knew that St. Joseph needed to keep up with the times and that the kids needed to know about the reality of what was happening in the world rather than be isolated from it.

A lot of people, a lot of priests, didn't like the way Father Frank was handling things. They complained to Bishop Saunders that Father Frank was teaching the kids about love and liberation and self-expression when he should have focused on teaching them the catechism and the rites and rituals of the Catholic Church.

Bishop Saunders wasn't happy to hear about Father Frank's approach. St. Joseph Seminary was his legacy, and he didn't want it tarnished. His solution was to remove Father Frank and the rest of the teachers and bring in an entirely new group of ultra-conservative priests.

Suddenly the kids were back to wearing black suits, white shirts, black ties, waking up to the sounds of bells in the hall, and having morning prayer in Latin at six o'clock.

Of course, you know what's going to happen when you take a fairly liberal high school and make it ultra-conservative. It's a big change. Kids leave, and then new kids hear what's going on and don't want to come.

Bishop Saunders realized in less than two years that he'd made a huge mistake by replacing Father Frank and his staff. He watched enrollment plummet, and he realized he needed to do something quickly or the school would never survive. But he was in a tough spot since he didn't want to draw attention to more big changes. He had to change the direction of the school once again, but he needed to keep it as quiet as possible.

The bishop met with Father Seth Tillman, a wonderful priest (and my best friend back then), and the two of them spent almost a year secretly making a plan to repair the damage at St. Joseph.

Bishop Saunders asked Seth to accept the job of director and to put together a faculty that could resurrect St. Joseph. Seth was liberal, just like Father Frank, the first director, had been. St. Joseph had gone from ultra-liberal to ultra-conservative in eight years, and now it was headed back to where it had started.

Seth called me and three other priests and asked us if we would like to be part of the new faculty at St. Joseph. I was still in Alexandria teaching high school religion and working at Catholic Services, and I had just finished my master's degree in secondary education.

There would be five of us—me, Seth, and three others. We couldn't tell a soul, because the existing faculty at St. Joseph had no idea that we would be coming to replace them. I'll never forget when it was all finalized. Bishop Saunders invited the five of us to a celebratory dinner meeting at the Washington Hotel in downtown Fairview. We met in one of the formal dining rooms, the kind with linen napkins on the tables and velvet drapes on the windows. That's when he officially appointed us as the new faculty at St. Joseph. We had two months to prepare.

St. Joseph had one hundred and fifty-six students enrolled when Father Frank left, and enrollment had dropped to fifty-two in two years. Most of the upperclassmen had left, and the word had spread about how rigid the school had become, so freshman enrollment was way down.

Our first job was to engage with the kids, to make the place more appealing—more human—and then to build enrollment. When we arrived, we lived in the guest rooms so we could connect with the outgoing faculty and learn the logistics—where the light switches were, how to operate the intercom system, things like that. We were all together for two weeks, two faculties there at the same time, one observing and the other finishing up and preparing to leave. That wasn't a pleasant two weeks.

The reality is that none of us had any experience running a boys' high school. I was the only one with any actual teaching experience, and even that was limited to teaching a couple of religion classes at the Catholic high school in Alexandria.

Somewhere along the line, we connected with a psychiatrist, and the six of us went out to dinner with him to try and get some insight into how to make the whole thing work. I don't know which one of us had a connection with him or how we ended up meeting with him. I don't even remember his name. I do remember the group having dinner with him one night at a little roadside diner near the school, and he said he would be willing to meet with us a few times to give us some ideas of how to run an all-boys high school.

We learned a lot from him. He hammered in that we couldn't just have a teacher/staff relationship with these kids. We needed to be like their older brothers at the same time. The kids were basically fourteen to eighteen years old, ninth grade through twelfth. I was twenty-eight, but I looked like I was about twenty, so it was easy for the kids to look at me and envision me as an older brother.

So, there we were, this group of five young priests, trying to play every role you can think of for fifty-two teenage boys. We were teacher, parent, brother, spiritual advisor all-in-one at this Catholic all-boys high school in the middle of nowhere.

And beyond our academic world was the real world: the Vietnam War, rioting in the streets, Woodstock, and free love. That was the culture. There was a lot of change going on, a lot of confusion for all of us. Sometimes it was hard to balance the relationships you had with these kids.

We opened that year with only eleven kids in the freshman class, about twenty-five percent of what we should have had. We had no way of recruiting new students for that first year because everything had been kept secret. Once the word got out that there was a new staff at St. Joseph, it was big news in the diocese, so we hoped that would boost enrollment for our second year. We needed a pretty enormous boost, because we had this massive building that was filled with empty space.

We had an infirmary, but it wasn't staffed. It wasn't practical, financially, to have a doctor on staff, or even a nurse. I often wished we had been able to have had a nurse, at least, because it seemed like every time I turned around, one of the kids needed some sort of medical attention.

Sometimes it was as simple as putting a bandage on a cut or ice on a twisted ankle, which we could handle. But those times when it was more serious, like when a dozen kids came down with the flu, that's when we needed a doctor to step in. Of course, if it was an emergency, then we'd drive to the emergency room at St. Elizabeth's Hospital in town. Luckily, that didn't happen often, and we never had a situation bad enough that we had to call an ambulance.

We were fortunate that one of the staff doctors from St. Elizabeth's lived not too far from the school, and since he drove right past St. Joseph on his way home, he was always willing to stop by if we needed him. We didn't need him often, but it was nice to know we could call when we did. He even kept some routine medicine and supplies in a locked cabinet in the infirmary—aspirin, antibiotics, bandages, that type of thing, so he'd have what he needed on hand. The staff had a key to the cabinet, but we were under strict orders to only open it if he gave us permission.

The property was gorgeous. The main building, all brick, was huge and made up of classrooms, dorm rooms, priests' rooms, guest rooms, and a chapel.

There was also a private house on the grounds that the bishop used for his summer home, and it had a gigantic swimming pool with decorative lights and beautiful landscaping. On scorching-hot nights, the kids would ask if they could go swimming, so we'd walk them down to the pool and wait for them. They were a bunch of teenage boys, obviously there were no girls around, and sometimes they wanted to go skinny dipping. It was one of those things that wasn't a big deal at the time.

The main building was only partially air-conditioned. The chapel was air-conditioned, of course, and that encouraged people to be in there. The faculty lounge was joined to the faculty dining room, and both of those rooms were air-conditioned as well.

Seth worked it out so that each priest had a sitting room, a bedroom, and a private bathroom in between those two rooms. He bought ten window unit air conditioners and put one in each of our living rooms and bedrooms.

There were three dorms for the students, and each one had space for fifty beds, which was a lot more than we needed at the time. The dorms weren't air-conditioned.

It can get painfully hot in Virginia, even into September. Sometimes it would be so blistering hot that the kids couldn't sleep. It wouldn't be unusual at all for one of us priests to hear a knock on our door at ten or eleven o'clock at night and find a couple of kids standing there asking to watch television in our sitting room because it was too hot for them to sleep.

When we went to bed, we'd tell the kids to keep the volume down on the television and turn it off when they were finished watching it. There were only three channels back then, and most broadcasts were over by eleven-thirty. There was a bathroom separating the sitting room from the bedroom, plus the air conditioner buzzed like the dickens, so you didn't hear the kids in the sitting room when you were in your bedroom.

I remember so many times waking up in the morning and walking into the sitting room to see two kids sound asleep on the floor and another one stretched out on the couch. Back then, we didn't think anything of it. There's no way you could do that in today's world.

CHAPTER FIVE

DISTANT MEMORIES

Any of you who lacks wisdom must ask God,
who gives to all generously and without scolding; it will be given.

But the prayer must be made with faith, and no trace of doubt,
because a person who has doubts is like the waves thrown up
in the sea by the buffeting of the wind.

~ JAMES 1:5-6

Of the five of us who went to staff St. Joseph, I was the only one with a graduate degree in education (I had a master's), so I was named principal. To meet accreditation standards, the principal had to have a graduate degree in education. Seth dealt with the daily operations of the school in general, and I dealt with the things that involved the kids. It was like he was President, and I was Dean of Students. I kept Seth in the loop with what was going on, but he wasn't as involved with the issues that crept up with the kids on a day-to-day basis as I was. Most of the time, the things I had to deal with were pretty simple: he said this, he took that from me without asking, that type of thing. Sometimes, though, one of the kids would show up in your office and say something that really surprised you.

There was one time I'll never forget. I was in my office. It was around the middle of January, and a kid knocked on the door. When he came in, he looked like his world had ended.

I said, "Hey, what's the matter, Daniel? You look pretty serious."

"Well, it's pretty bad, Father. I think I've got syphilis."

"What makes you think you have syphilis? And how in the world would you have gotten it?" This was one of the times I really wished we'd had a nurse on-site.

"I went on a date." He said the date had been around Christmas when he'd gone home for the break.

"Well, what'd you do on that date? Did you have intercourse?"

"No, no, no." He shook his head until I thought it would fall off of his shoulders. "Nothing like that. We just kissed. That's it. But now I have this bump. It showed up yesterday."

I told him I didn't think he could have gotten syphilis from a kiss. He was fifteen, and it surprised me that he didn't know that. The next thing I knew, he had pulled his pants down and was standing there pointing to this tiny bump on his penis.

"That's why you think you have syphilis? Does it hurt? Does it itch?"

"No, Father."

"Then how did you even know it was there? I can barely see it."

"I saw it when I went to the bathroom. It wasn't there before."

I told him that those things happened sometimes, and it would probably go away in a few days. If it didn't go away soon or if it started to bother him, then we would call the doctor. That was the end of it. He left my office and never said another word about his syphilis.

The point here is that there wasn't a lot of modesty. I think part of it was the time, late sixties and early seventies, and part of it was the culture at the school. There were a bunch of teenage boys living with a handful of young priests who were trying to balance being their teachers with being their friends, their big brothers, their parents.

Part of our job was to turn the school around, to make it more "human." We needed to loosen the reins on the kids so that the ones who were there would stay, and also so that we could recruit others to enroll. It was a delicate balance, trying to come up with creative ways to run a seminary while allowing the kids to have fun at the same time.

One thing we came up with was an annual spiritual retreat at the beach, which was about a two-hour drive from the school. Typically, when seminary students went on retreat, they sat in a room and just listened for hours on end—lecture, benediction, praying the Rosary, more lecture. The students sat, and the facilitators talked. Normal retreats weren't very interactive, and they certainly weren't what a teenage boy would call fun.

We decided to rent some houses on the beach and do our retreats a different way. We'd pile the kids into a big rental van and make the drive to the beach. Once we got there, we'd move the furniture around to make room for movie projectors and all the other things we brought. The goal was to make it interactive and fun.

There were too many kids, even in the first few years, to take them all at the same time. So, two of the priests and I would take half of them on Sunday and come back to St. Joseph on Tuesday. Wednesday was a break for me, because I was exhausted after three days of supervising kids at the beach. Then two other priests and I would do it all again Thursday through Saturday.

We always went on our retreats in February, although that seems like an odd month to go to the beach since February is about the coldest month of the year in Virginia. We chose February because beach houses are cheap at that time of year. It gets dark early, and it's so cold that most people would never go to the beach in the dead of winter. But the kids didn't seem to mind it; in fact, they seemed to have a great time every year.

We'd always take them out for dinner the first night to a little family-owned Italian restaurant a few blocks away. It was one of the few places at the beach that stayed open year-round.

I remember one year we came back from dinner and built a fire in the fireplace. We got a pretty good burn going, and it started to get hot in the house. There was a big, wrap-around deck, so we all went outside to cool off a bit. We stood there looking at the sky, no one saying a word. It was just a beautiful, clear night.

All of a sudden, one of the kids bellowed, "Let's go streaking!"

They all looked at me as if they were waiting for my reaction. Even the other teachers just stood there staring at me.

Well, there wasn't a soul around in any of the other houses, so there was no one to see them but us. It was February, dark and freezing cold, so going streaking was a pretty stupid idea. But they were teenage boys, and teenage boys sometimes have stupid ideas.

I remember saying, "I'm not going to tell you that you can go streaking. But I'm going inside. What you do after that is up to you." I thought it was harmless, and I didn't see any reason to stop them.

I went inside, the other teachers followed me in, and the boys went streaking. I'm sure it was a sight to behold with a dozen of them running down the beach naked in the freezing cold. They didn't last long. About five minutes later, they all burst through the door and pulled on their clothes.

That was the kind of thing that happened when you had a bunch of teenage boys who just wanted to act like teenage boys. We gave them a lot of freedom, but within reason. They were even allowed to smoke as long as they had their parents' permission, but smoking wasn't as taboo then as it is now.

We didn't have serious discipline problems, at least for the first few years. The real problems started about the fourth year I was there, so that would have been in the early 1970s. That's when drugs started creeping into the school. It was addressed quickly every time we became aware of a problem; we even threw some kids out because of drug use. We thought we had a good handle on the drug issue, and we tried to deal with it, but apparently the problem was much more widespread than I realized at the time.

We were naïve, the faculty and staff, when it came to these types of things, and I'm sure there was a lot going on that we missed. Some of the kids were pretty ingenious when it came to sneaking things past us, so they probably got away with more than we'll ever know.

It wasn't until years after St. Joseph closed that I found out how much drug use went on right under our noses. We had no clue. Even some of the theater kids, the ones I spent a lot of time with outside of class, were using drugs. One kid in particular, Ryan Williams, who had been in all of the plays, really involved in a lot of things at the school, was, according to his classmates, high as a kite almost the whole time he was there. How we, the staff, never knew is beyond me.

It feels so odd now to think about these kids streaking and smoking and skinny dipping all those decades ago. Back then, that's just the type of stuff they did. They weren't bad kids, and for the most part, they didn't do bad things. The drug use was bad, of course, but we dealt with it as best we could. I think most of them enjoyed their time there at St. Joseph; it was a sort of brotherhood, almost like a fraternity for high school boys.

The staff lived on-site all year-round. We'd spend the summer recovering from the school year and preparing for the next year. The summer months were when we had repairs and maintenance done on the buildings and grounds.

The kids went home during the summer, but it wasn't unusual to have a few of the students call and ask if they could come back and stay for a few weeks to earn extra money. Some of them weren't old enough to get *actual* jobs back at home, so they would work at the school, painting, landscaping, things like that. The kids were pretty innovative, too. They would paint inside at night when it was cooler, and they'd usually go swimming after they finished working. Then they'd go to bed really late, sometimes in the early morning hours, and sleep until late in the day. They'd wake up in time to eat lunch, sometimes dinner, then start it all over again.

The staff didn't care what the kids' schedules were in the summer as long as they did what they were supposed to do and didn't cause any problems. Their parents were thrilled because it kept them out of trouble and out of their hair for part of the summer. The boys were happy because they earned some spending money, and the staff was happy because we had inexpensive labor.

We had a diverse group of kids at St. Joseph as far as their parents' income levels. At one extreme were the kids whose parents were millionaires, and at the other extreme were the kids who were there on scholarship because their parents didn't have a dime.

The great thing about a boarding school is that they all wear the same uniforms, so you don't have a division based on social class. There wasn't much to spend money on while they were at school, so the differences didn't show up there, either. Two kids could have backgrounds as different as night and day, but at St. Joseph they lived like brothers, and they all got along pretty well for the most part.

The gesture of peace at Mass took between ten and fifteen minutes. As long as we had two priests celebrating Mass together, that ten to fifteen-minute period was enough time for me to sneak into the sanctuary, have a cigarette, and get back to see everybody hugging and apologizing.

"I'm sorry I said you were an asshole."

"I'm sorry I called you a son of a bitch."

"I took your toothpaste, that's why you couldn't find it yesterday."

They'd hug each other and apologize for everything under the sun. I don't think you see that as much today, but that's what we tried to teach them: forgiveness and acceptance.

There were three different groups of students at St. Joseph: the theater kids, the jocks, and then everybody else. Theater was always my thing, so the theater kids naturally gravitated towards me. We put on two plays each year, one in the late fall and one in the late spring. There's one that stands out. I think the name of it was *Child's Play*. I had seen it on Broadway around 1970, and I knew we had to do this play at St. Joseph.

It's basically the story of a priest who's everybody's buddy. The story ironically took place at a boys' boarding school. The main character, the priest, let them get away with all kinds of things—nothing sexual, more along the lines of violence—and the priest did nothing to stop them. Another character was a coach who the kids didn't like because he was tough on them.

There's a scene where one of the students is found murdered. A priest found his dead body sprawled across a statue of the Pietà, the Michelangelo sculpture with Jesus lying across Mary's lap. We had a replica of that statue in one of the buildings: wooden, beautifully carved, and painted a glossy, creamy white. It was about seven feet tall and must have weighed close to five hundred pounds. How we were able to get that statue on that stage in one piece I don't remember, but somehow, we did it.

There were four or five non-speaking parts, and Ryan Williams, the kid with the drug problem, and his best friend, David Baxter, had two of those parts. Williams played the part of the student who was found dead lying across the Pietà. Baxter played the part of the priest. He walked into the room, wearing a clerical collar, and found the dead student, bloody and shirtless.

CHAPTER SIX

THE REASSIGNMENTS

Yes, I know what plans I have in mind for you, Yahweh declares,
plans for peace, not for disaster, to give you a future and a hope.

When you call to me and come and pray to me, I shall listen to you.

When you search for me, you will find me;
when you search wholeheartedly for me,

I shall let you find me (Yahweh declares. I shall restore
your fortunes and gather you in from all the nations
and wherever I have driven you, Yahweh declares.
I shall bring you back to the from which I exiled you).

~ JEREMIAH 29:11-14

My ten years at St. Joseph went by pretty quickly; I stayed there as principal until they shut down in 1978. We'd done a pretty good job recruiting kids the first few years, but by the late 1970s there wasn't much interest in an all-boys seminary, so enrollment had dropped to the point where the diocese couldn't afford to keep the doors open.

After St. Joseph closed, the bishop sent me to a coastal town in the eastern part of the state, Mooresville, to open a new parish. I was in Mooresville for only a year, just long enough to get the Church of the Resurrection started. It was a totally new experience for me, opening a new parish, and it was thrilling. I felt like I had found my passion. But my parents were starting to have some health problems by that point, so after a year, I asked for a transfer so that I could be closer to them in Fairview.

The bishop was planning to open another new parish on the south side of Fairview, only about twenty minutes from my parents' house. He sent me there to open St. Francis Xavier Catholic Church. I loved being back in my hometown. I reconnected with old friends, and I formed lots of new friendships with the parishioners.

My time at St. Francis Xavier was wonderful, but priests don't normally stay at one parish for too many years. I was there for eight years, which is pretty normal. I left in 1987. By this time, both of my parents had passed away. The biggest blessing of my entire life came from being at St. Francis Xavier, where I met Adeline. She answered a classified advertisement that I placed in the *Daily Times* when I was looking for a church secretary. Adeline's children were in high school, and she was looking for something to fill her time. I hired her to be my secretary, but she became my best friend, my confidante. We were almost exactly the same age, but she looked out for me as if I were her son.

My next assignment was back to the coast. I went to Hamilton County to serve as principal of Hamilton Catholic High School. I was there for five years until 1992. By that time, Bishop Saunders had retired, and Bishop Thomas Robertson had taken his place. Robertson and Saunders were as different as night and day. Bishop Saunders was very regal. He was always in control, very much put together, both in his appearance and in his mannerisms. He was guarded, harsh, and firm. Saunders was completely no nonsense.

Bishop Robertson, on the other hand, was very laid back, very loose. *Malleable* is probably the best word to describe him. He was easy to sway if you wanted him to do something for you or if you wanted to change his mind about something. The priests in the Diocese of Fairfield learned pretty quickly that if they wanted something from Robertson, they could take him out for dinner, give him a couple of drinks, and he'd likely warm up to almost anything they asked him to do. You couldn't ask for the moon, but if you wanted a little increase in the budget or if you wanted a new assignment somewhere else in the diocese, then those types of things were pretty easy to get from him. Robertson was good about give-and-take. If he asked you to do something, you could usually negotiate with him to get something you wanted in return. That's how I ended up at St. Edward Catholic Church in 1992.

While I was principal of Hamilton Catholic, Bishop Robertson announced that the school would be moving to a different county the following year, about an hour up the coast. After spending ten years as principal at St. Joseph and another five at Hamilton, I needed a permanent break from being a high school principal. I told Robertson that I wanted to be assigned to a parish, preferably a parish close to Fairview.

The timing was perfect. Robertson had bought a piece of land in Springfield, a town just west of Fairview, a few years prior. His plan had been to build a co-educational Catholic middle and high school. He spent a few years trying to get that plan off the ground, but by 1992 he realized that the demand wasn't there for the school. However, there was plenty of demand for a new parish in Springfield.

Robertson decided to build a church on the land instead of a school, and he asked me to move to Springfield and start the parish. I was only in my fifties, but I wanted St. Edward to be my last assignment. That would mean staying there for close to twenty years, which is almost unheard of for a parish priest. I made a deal with Robertson. I'd start St. Edward if he'd promise not to reassign me as long as he was bishop of Fairfield. He agreed, so off I went to finish my days as a priest at St. Edward.

I loved being back home, close to Fairview. I reconnected with my parishioner friends from St. Francis Xavier and was able to spend time with my brothers since they both still lived there. The best part was reconnecting with Adeline. She was still working as the secretary at St. Francis Xavier, but it didn't take much to convince her to leave and come with me to St. Edward. She was so much more than a secretary at St. Edward; Adeline was the cornerstone of the church.

The first year was a blur of recruiting and fundraising. You can't fundraise without parishioners, and you can't get parishioners unless you recruit. I went to all the parishes within a thirty-minute drive of where St. Edward would be built and held meetings, like town halls, to tell people about St. Edward in hopes that they'd leave their parishes and help me open the new one. Of course, the priests at those parishes weren't crazy about that, since I was trying to entice their parishioners to leave. But that's the way it worked when a new parish opened, so they had no choice but to go along with it.

We started St. Edward with about thirty-five people. We rented space at a middle school and held our one Sunday morning Mass there. There was a Methodist church about a mile away from where our church building would be built, and the minister there was kind enough to allow us to celebrate Mass there on Saturday evenings. It took us about three years to raise the money we needed in order for the diocese to allow us to break ground on the building. The diocese required us to have one-third on hand in cash, another third in pledges, and they would get a mortgage for the balance needed for construction. It took another fifteen months to complete construction. We opened the doors in mid-1996 with about four hundred families registered. That's when our numbers began to grow. While the church was being constructed, so many people said, "We'll join St. Edward when the church is built." Well, we built a church, and they joined. We had almost six hundred registered families by the end of the year.

The numbers kept growing every month. But I didn't want a parish filled with people who just showed up every Sunday and then you never saw them again until the next week. I wanted a parish filled with people who really wanted to be *there* at *that* parish, so I made sure that people had to jump through a few hoops in order to register.

We had newcomer meetings every month, one after Mass on Sunday and one in the evening during the week; you couldn't join the parish until you went to a meeting. We'd hand out forms at the meetings and have everyone fill them out to tell us what ministry they were willing to join. We expected everyone who joined the parish to participate in some way.

My goal wasn't to have a huge parish; it was to have a parish filled with active people who made a difference in our town. I wanted us to have a real impact on the community. My motto was *who will miss us if we're gone?*

I was lucky to have a great core group of people who helped me get the parish started, and they did a wonderful job of leading the way toward a parish full of active, engaged parishioners. St. Edward ran like a well-oiled machine.

Besides me, Adeline was the only employee in the beginning, but soon I had a small staff and a group of volunteers who ran the place. I was able to do what I loved—weddings, baptisms, counseling, those types of things. I could minister to the people, which was what I did best, while Adeline kept everything running.

I was on top of the world for that first year at St. Edward. I felt settled, like I was finally at home, doing what I was meant to do. That all came to a halt in the summer of 1997, when I got a phone call from Father William Russell, Bill, telling me that Bishop Robertson wanted to see me immediately.

Bill was the Vicar for Priests, so he was the one who had to deal with problems that came up involving any priest in our diocese. If there was a rumor floating around that a priest was drinking too much or preaching about something that wasn't quite in line with the teachings of the Church, then Bill would step in and figure out what was going on. I couldn't imagine why Bill was calling me and telling me to go straight to see the bishop.

CHAPTER SEVEN

THE FIRST ONE

If we say that we share in God's life while we are living in darkness,
we are lying, because we are not living the truth.

But if we live in light, as he is in light, we have a share in another's
life, and the blood of Jesus, his Son, cleanses us from all sin.

If we say, 'We have no sin,' we are deceiving ourselves,
and truth has no place in us;

if we acknowledge our sins, he is trustworthy and upright,
so that he will forgive our sins and will cleanse us from all evil.

If we say, 'We have never sinned,' we make him a liar,
and his word has no place in us.

~ JOHN 1:6-10

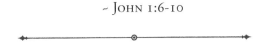

I remember exactly what day it was when Bill called because it was the Feast of Mary Magdalene, so it would have been July 22, a Tuesday. I asked Adeline to cancel my appointments and drove fifteen minutes to the chancery to see the bishop. His secretary was out that day, and the door to his office was open, as if he were waiting for me.

When I walked into his office, he told me to sit down, that he had something important to discuss with me.

"Paul, do you remember a student at St. Joseph named Ryan Williams?"

Even though it had been over twenty years since I'd seen him, I remembered Williams. "He'd been one of the theater kids," I replied. "And I think he was one of the students who worked around the property during the summers."

"I have a letter from Williams that I think you should see. It came in the mail Friday afternoon."

Bishop Robertson handed me an envelope, postmarked a few days prior. I opened it and was shocked by what I was reading. Williams wrote that I had sexually assaulted him back in the 1970s when he was a student at St. Joseph. He went into great detail about all kinds of things that he said I did to him, from fondling to rape. He said that another student, David Baxter, was involved as well.

In the letter, Williams claimed that he remembered being on the floor of the stage in the theater, lying down, with me hovering over him. He said I was wearing my clerical collar, and that Baxter was there and was part of the whole thing. He described all sorts of sexual things that he said the three of us were doing with each other, that it continued into the summer when he and Baxter came to the school to work, and that it went on for the entire four years that he was a student at St. Joseph.

Williams said that he had suppressed the memories, but then he read an article in the *Virginia Catholic* a month before about me and the opening of St. Edward, and the memories suddenly came flooding back. He told the bishop to track down David Baxter, and that Baxter would confirm the entire story.

"Paul, can you please explain this to me?" The bishop looked at me as if I might actually have answers.

"No, I can't explain that!" I bellowed. "That's the craziest thing I've ever heard! I don't remember too much about Ryan Williams, but I can promise you that none of that ever happened! Clearly, he's either a liar or he's crazy, and after reading that letter it sounds to me like he might be both."

What Williams described in the letter sounded a lot like the scene from one of the plays we put on at St. Joseph, the one with the statue of the Pietà. Williams had played the character who had been found dead; Baxter had played the part of the priest, wearing a clerical collar, standing over him.

I explained all of that to Robertson and told him that it sounded like Williams' memory was of the play, because the sexual abuse he described in the letter had never happened.

Williams said in his letter that if the bishop sent him a million dollars, the whole thing would go away, but if he didn't pay, then Williams would go to the newspapers with his story. This was right about the time that Catholic dioceses all over the country were paying out millions of dollars to settle sexual abuse cases. It seemed like every day there was another article in the newspaper about a multi-million-dollar settlement somewhere in a diocese in the United States.

"I spoke with Williams on the phone yesterday. He told me exactly the same thing that he wrote in the letter, and he insists that it's all true. He sounds very convincing; I'll give him that." This statement came from the man who could be convinced of anything. It's a good thing Williams didn't send him a bottle of scotch; the bishop would believe anything he said then.

"Of course, he sounded convincing! I'd sound convincing, too, if I were trying to get you to give me a million dollars! Bishop, I'm certainly no saint, but I DID NOT DO ANY OF THIS!"

"Calm down, Paul. I can't imagine that you'd do anything like that, but I can't just let this thing go. I have an obligation as the bishop of this diocese to investigate this. I'll have Bill look into it and see what he comes up with. He's the one who should take charge of this, anyway. And Paul, let's keep this between us for now. There's no reason to tell anyone else besides Bill about this right now. Do you agree?"

"Yes, agreed. Who would I tell?" Looking back, having to keep all of that a secret had been harder than I thought it would be. Having someone to confide in would have helped, but that hadn't been an option.

The Catholic Church was under so much scrutiny already, with accusations of priests sexually abusing minors making the newspaper headlines almost daily. The last thing Robertson wanted was for the media to find out about it, so he was trying to keep it as quiet as possible.

When accusations like this happened, the diocese obviously had to take them seriously, and deep down I understood that. I just never expected this to happen to me. Bishop Robertson had no choice but to start an investigation. Since he'd already heard Ryan Williams' side, the next step was to speak with David Baxter.

Bill Russell was able to track down Baxter pretty easily; he only lived a few hours away from the diocesan offices. Bill scheduled a meeting, and he drove to meet Baxter and showed him the letter.

According to Bill, Baxter read the letter and said the whole thing was a lie, that he had never witnessed anything like that and he never even went to St. Joseph in the summer. He also told Bill that Ryan Williams had a big drug problem in high school, and he always wondered why the staff at St. Joseph never figured that out. He said that Williams was high most of the time when he was in high school.

Bill came back and gave his report to the bishop. But considering everything going on with Catholic priests at the time, Bishop Robertson still couldn't let it go. I didn't blame him, although in reality I thought it was ridiculous to go any further with this.

The bishop's next step was to send me to see a psychiatrist who specialized in sexual abuse crimes. I spent more hours with him than I can count, throughout August and most of September. The psychiatrist sent a report to the bishop that said, basically, there was nothing he could come up with in his analysis of me that indicated I was capable of sexual assault. He was regarded as an expert in his field, and specifically with issues of this nature, so the bishop felt he could put the situation to rest.

Robertson sent Williams a certified letter to tell him his findings, the denial from David Baxter, the result of the psychiatric assessment, and that the diocese would not be paying him the million dollars.

There was no more word from Williams after that; he didn't go to the newspapers and didn't contact the bishop again. He seemed to have disappeared as quickly as he had shown up. It had been a hellish couple of months, but I thought it was over.

Life was wonderful for the next five years.

CHAPTER EIGHT

ONCE AGAIN

My child, if you aspire to serve the Lord,
prepare yourself for an ordeal.

Be sincere of heart, be steadfast,
and do not be alarmed when disaster comes.

Cling to him and do not leave him,
so that you may be honoured at the end of your days.

Whatever happens to you, accept it,
and in the uncertainties of your humble state, be patient,

since gold is tested in the fire,
and the chosen in the furnace of humiliation.

Trust him and he will uphold you,
follow a straight path and hope in him.

~ SIRACH 2:1-6

I had thought that this was over, this stuff with Ryan Williams. His accusation had lurked in the back of my mind, but it certainly didn't keep me awake at night. The nightmare returned five years later, in 2002, on a Tuesday morning in April, not long after Easter.

"Father," Adeline said, "I left a message for you on your desk from Bishop Robertson. It was on the answering machine when I got to work this morning, so it must have come in early. Judging from the sound of his voice, it must be important."

Adeline insisted on calling me *Father*, although I'd told her more times than I could remember that she could certainly call me *Paul*. It always seemed odd for my best friend to be so formal with me. But she was a true old-school Catholic, and there was no way she would ever call a priest by his first name, no matter how close the relationship.

The message was written on one of those pink squares of paper, that kind that has *While You Were Out* printed across the top. The time noted was seven forty-five, and at the bottom, in broad cursive handwriting, Adeline wrote: *Bishop Robertson says to call him immediately. He says it's very important.*

I dialed the chancery, and the bishop's secretary, Norma, put me right through, but without her normal cheerful comments about the weather or some other benign topic.

"I need to see you tomorrow morning at ten o'clock here in my office." There was no greeting, no chit-chat.

"About what?" I hoped that perhaps a disgruntled parishioner hadn't liked something I said in my homily last weekend, and the bishop wanted me to come in so I could get a verbal slap on the hand. Deep down, though, I knew that it was much more than that.

"I can't tell you." That was it, then silence.

That seemed more than a little odd. "Well, you can give me some hint, can't you? I mean, am I in trouble? What's all this urgency, this secrecy, about?"

"Can't tell you, can't tell you. Just be here at ten tomorrow." Then he hung up the phone.

I sat there for a moment, trying to process the conversation. I knew it was serious, and I was fairly certain that it was bad, whatever it was. I was starting to panic, so I called Bill Russell, the Vicar for Priests. First, I called his office and then his cell phone. I left messages at both numbers.

"Bill, you need to call me. The bishop wants to see me. He says it's important. I don't know whether it's good or bad. Sounds like it's more bad than good to me." I called him three times in an hour; he never called me back.

An hour later, I called Gregory Johns. Greg was a priest with a Ph.D. in clinical psychology. He worked with Bill on the diocesan assessment team—that's the group that steps in when a priest is having an issue that needs to be handled. There were three people on the team, all priests. The third one was Clarke Harlow, a licensed clinical social worker. If there was a complaint about a priest, it was his job to figure out what was going on and then to make recommendations to the bishop about how to handle it.

I called Greg. No answer, so I left a message. I called again and left another message. Like Bill, he never returned my calls.

I did my best to go about my day as I normally would, but I felt too sick to concentrate or function. By lunchtime, I knew there was no use in trying to do anything, so I told Adeline to cancel my afternoon appointments because I was going home and wouldn't be back until the next afternoon.

Walking usually clears my head, but it didn't help. I had no appetite, just a pit in my stomach as if something terrible were about to happen. Adeline called to check on me, but I lied and told her I was fine. I tried to sleep that night, but it didn't happen. My imagination conjured up all kinds of crazy reasons why the bishop would be acting so strangely.

But every thought I had came back to Ryan Williams. I tried not to let myself think about it, to tell myself that the mystery meeting with Robertson could be about anything. It was no use. My thoughts were consumed with fear that Williams was back.

The next morning, I made a decision. I needed advice from a friend. Maybe this was about Williams; maybe not. But Robertson didn't tell me *this time* that I had to keep things secret, and I had to talk to someone I could trust.

I called Wayne Michaels on the way to the chancery. Wayne was a parishioner at St. Edward and was more like a buddy to me. Wayne and I had met at St. Joseph thirty-odd years ago; he was a student, a freshman, the year that I became principal.

Wayne and his wife, Marla, were founding members at St. Francis Xavier, which was how we reconnected years after he graduated from St Joseph. They both played a big part in getting the parish started, and our friendship involved activities such as having dinner together or going to the movies.

When I left St. Francis Xavier, I stayed in touch with them, and we would get together whenever I came back to Fairview for a visit. After Bishop Robertson sent me to Springfield to start St. Edward, Wayne and Marla left St. Francis Xavier and joined me. It was about a thirty-minute trip from their home on the south side of Fairview, and it thrilled me they were willing to make the drive.

Wayne and Marla began to have problems about two years after we started St. Edward, and eventually they divorced. Wayne had come to me for counseling when he and Marla were trying to work out their problems before deciding to end their marriage. You get to know someone pretty well when you're walking with them through a rough journey, and that's when Wayne and I became close friends. Wayne was one of the two people whom I knew I could always count on; Adeline was the other.

Luckily, Wayne answered my call right away that morning. After exchanging pleasantries, I told him that the bishop had called an urgent meeting with me, and I was worried.

"He wouldn't tell me what it's about, but I know it's bad."

"If he didn't tell you what it's about, then how do you know it's bad?" Wayne asked in his reasonable way.

"I can tell, I just know."

"You always do this, assume the worst. It could be anything. I'm betting someone got pissed off last Sunday about something you said and now Robertson wants to slap your hand and tell you not to do it again."

That was typical Wayne.

Funny thing was, that had been my first thought, too, until the nightmare from five years ago dampened that hope. Of course, this wasn't something I could easily explain to Wayne, as I had never confided in him about the situation with Ryan Williams.

"Yes, I'm sure you're right," I said, hoping I sounded like I agreed with him and was brushing off my own concern. "Thanks for setting me straight."

I got to the chancery and was glad to see that Norma, Bishop Robertson's secretary, was there that day. Norma knew everything that happened in the diocese, usually before anyone else. I stopped at her desk, which was just outside of the bishop's office. Everyone had to go through Norma to see the bishop. His office door was open once again that morning, but this time only a crack.

Unlike the day before on the phone, that day she was her typical self. "Come over here and let me hug you! How've you been? He'll be with you in a minute. He's finishing up a call with Bishop Walters."

Out of the corner of my eye, I could see through the crack of the door that Bishop Robertson was on the phone. He appeared to be whispering, holding the phone in his left hand while his right hand was cupped over his mouth.

I wondered what he and Carl Walters were discussing. My assumption was that it had to do with Walters' recent appointment as Robertson's auxiliary bishop and his impending arrival in Fairview. I had never cared for Walters, so I wasn't eager to work with him, but that was probably the least of my concerns at that moment.

Bishop Robertson walked out of his office. "Come on, Paul, we're going across the street to the house."

The 'house' he was referring to was the bishop's private residence, which was right across the street from the bishop's office, the chancery. The Cathedral was located next to the chancery, with the three buildings forming an inner-city triangle of Catholicism.

"Why are we going to the house? What's this all about?" That pit in my stomach returned, and I sensed something awful was about to happen. Nausea hit suddenly, and I thought I was going to throw up.

Bishop Robertson didn't say a word until we were outside, standing on the sidewalk.

"It's pretty bad. In fact, it doesn't get any worse." He strolled across the street toward the house, as if he had all day.

I broke out in a cold sweat. "Well, what is it? What's with all the secrecy? It's so bad that we can't even discuss it at the chancery?" By then, my composure was just about gone. I turned the ring on my hand, a nervous habit I've had for as long as I can remember. I was sweating so much that the ring nearly fell to the street.

"I'll tell you. I'll tell you. Let's just get to the house." He continued to walk at a snail's pace, which was infuriating me.

The three-minute walk seemed like it took an hour, but we finally made it across the street to the bishop's house. There was a small parlor to the left just as you walked through the front door, and just ahead was a staircase that went up to the bishop's private quarters. To the left of the stairs, a set of double doors led to a spacious living room and behind that was a huge dining room. Everything was ornate, baroque even, with dark, intricately carved wood everywhere you looked.

The bishop put me in that little parlor, shut the door, and disappeared. No explanation, not a word. Then, a few minutes later, he came back. "There's been an accusation."

Finally, the secrecy was starting to make sense, but this was extreme. "What kind of accusation?"

"Well, you'll, you'll find out in a few minutes."

"You're not going to tell me anymore other than there's been an accusation?" I was about to explode at that point.

"No, well, no, you know, I don't want you to get the feeling like we're all here to gang up against you when you go into the living room."

Fury was taking over. I could feel my face flush beet-red, my hands forming fists as if I might actually pull a punch.

"Why would I feel that way? Who in the world is in the living room? Bishop, this makes no damn sense at all. I deserve an explanation!"

He then told me that Bill Russell, Gregory Johns, and Clarke Harlow were waiting for me in the living room along with another man whom I'd never heard of; he was a psychiatrist, not a priest.

We walked down the hall to the living room, and the four of them were sitting in a circle. I forced myself to walk around the room, shaking hands, returning their stiff hugs, the confusion and anger rising with each patronizing pat on the back, but I was still somehow managing to hold it together.

I reached Bill last, and by that time, the anger had taken over. "Where in the hell have you been? I've been trying to reach you for almost twenty-four hours! Dammit, Bill, I don't know what in the hell is going on here, but you could have had the decency to return my calls."

"Well, it's just one of those things. You know, we do things different-ly now after Jeff Stephens."

For Bill to bring up Father Jeffrey Stephens meant that the bishop was right; it was really bad.

PART TWO

THE END

I plead with you—never, ever give up on hope,
never doubt, never tire,

and never become discouraged. Be not afraid.

~ Pope John Paul II

CHAPTER NINE

CHANGE IN PROTOCOL

＋━━━━━━━◉━━━━━━━＋

Jesus, then, was brought before the governor,
and the governor put to him this question,
'Are you the king of the Jews?' Jesus replied, 'It is you who say it.'

But when he was accused by the chief priests
and the elders he refused to answer at all.

Pilate then said to him,
'Do you not hear how many charges they have made against you?'

But to the governor's amazement,
he offered not a word in answer to any of the charges.

~ MATTHEW 27:11-14

＋━━━━━━━◉━━━━━━━＋

In 1988, a group of parochial-school teachers at St. Patrick Catholic School in Fairview, Virginia, approached Bishop Theodore Saunders, then bishop of the Diocese of Fairview, with concerns about the behavior of twenty-seven-year-old Father Jeffrey Stephens.

They accused Stephens of abusing elementary school-aged boys in his sex education class by having them sit on his lap and feel his erect penis. The bishop responded to the accusations by reassigning Stephens to St. Margaret Catholic Church, a parish two hours away in the same diocese.

Eleven years later, in 1999, a young man, Clay Webster, committed suicide. Webster had attended St. Patrick in the mid to late 1980s and was a student of Father Stephens.

In planning Webster's funeral, his parents were adamant that Father Stephens, by that time assigned to St. Jude Catholic Church in the western part of the diocese, not take part in nor attend Webster's funeral Mass. This made its way back to Bishop Saunders, who questioned why the parents would not want one of their son's former teachers to attend his funeral. It was then that the parents told the bishop what the teachers had also told him eleven years prior; Stephens had allegedly sexually abused their son in the late 1980s. The bishop now felt a need to confront Father Stephens.

Six weeks later, on a Wednesday afternoon, the bishop told Father Stephens about the abuse allegations and scheduled a time to follow up with Stephens and open a diocesan investigation.

The following Saturday morning, Father Stephens committed suicide by a gunshot to the head. He left suicide notes to his mother and to the bishop, denying all of the accusations.

Since that time, the Catholic Diocese of Fairview has taken a different approach to both the handling of abuse allegations and the way that they notify the accused.

The air in the bishop's house was beginning to suffocate me. I was angry, nauseous, I couldn't breathe.

"Paul," Bishop Robertson began, "we've decided that you're going to Taylor Psychiatric Pavilion in Maryland for a full psychiatric evaluation. Bill will drive you to your place now to pack a bag, then he'll drive you up to Taylor Pavilion this afternoon. I've spoken to the director, and they're expecting you."

It sounded more like a question than a statement. Robertson sounded as confused as I felt, as if he were giving me an order, but at the same time wasn't quite sure what he was actually doing. The others just stood there, blank stares on their faces, as if they had no idea how this was supposed to play out. It was all very awkward and surreal.

Finally, I realized that no one was taking the lead here, so I decided that maybe I should. "Would someone tell me exactly what I'm accused of and who has accused me?"

They were all acting like confused children, not knowing what to do. "There's a, there's a…" stammered Robertson. "There's a letter that came a few days ago."

"Well, may I see it? I'm certainly allowed to read this letter, aren't I?" I had tried to calm down, but I was struggling.

They all looked around at each other as if no one knew if I was allowed to see the letter or not. It was the craziest thing, as if no one had a clue what was actually going on. They had brought me there to talk about this, yet I was the only one who seemed to want to say anything. I know I'll never have a nervous breakdown because if I didn't have one then, I never will.

Bill looked over at Bishop Robertson, who gave a slight nod of his head. Finally, Bill handed me the letter. As I had suspected by that point, the letter was from Ryan Williams, accusing me once again of the unimaginable.

This time he went into more details than he had five years ago. He claimed that I drugged him, and that I raped him while he was too out of it to stop me. He said that it went on the entire time he was at St. Joseph in the 1970s, over twenty years ago.

"This is insane! None of this ever happened! Ryan Williams tried this five years ago. I told you then, it never happened! Bishop, you checked it out then. You talked to the other kid who Williams said was part of it. He said it never happened. This whole thing is a lie! Bishop, I don't understand any of this, and I'm not going to just stand here and take it!"

"Oh, well, you know, of course I remember. What we're going to do with this is, well, we're going to send you for a full psychiatric evaluation, and then we'll see what we're going to do after that. You know, Paul, the letter is from his lawyer. This is serious this time."

Yes, I had seen that the letter was from an attorney. "It was serious last time! Maybe you'd think it was more serious if someone had accused you of rape, but this is about me! I'm not going to Taylor Pavilion or anywhere else, and you can't force me to go! But I am going to get a lawyer of my own!"

"Paul, you can't do that." Clearly, Bishop Robertson had lost his mind. "You, well, you have to go through the process the way we planned it. We have it all arranged with Taylor Pavilion. You're checking in tonight."

"I can't do that? Yes, I can do that! And no, I'm not doing it the way you planned. I am not going to Taylor Pavilion tonight! I'm going to get an attorney! If my attorney says I should go through your process, then maybe I'll go through the process. I will not be a puppet; this is MY life we're talking about! I know enough about psychological assessments that I know you don't have to go and stay at a residential facility; they can all be done as an outpatient. You can send me to a bunch of different psychiatrists with different specialties and see what they come up with. I know how this works. But I'm not doing anything unless my attorney says I should!"

Robertson looked even more confused. "You're trying to control this thing."

"Damn right, I'm trying to control it! Nobody else here seems to have control of it, and nobody seems to be trying to help me with it!"

I stood up, walked out of the house and to my car, and called Wayne and then Adeline on the drive home. They both met me at the rectory, and I broke down and told them about the letter and about everything that had happened five years ago when Ryan Williams first accused me.

I knew I had to get an attorney quickly. I was wishing that I'd gotten one five years ago, but it was too late to think about that. The only attorney that I knew personally was Peter Gowan, a parishioner at St. Francis Xavier. He had come to St. Edward for Mass a few months before all of this, and we went to lunch after to catch up. I didn't even know what type of law he practiced, but Adeline and I both felt like I could trust him to help. I called him and told him about the letter from Williams.

"Can you represent me? Or can you give me a reference?" I didn't know who I'd call if Peter said no.

"I'll call you back in 10 minutes."

It was probably the longest ten minutes of my life. I sat with Wayne and Adeline and talked about every *what if* scenario we could come up with. There was no good 'if.'

Finally, the phone rang. "Bob James is who you want. Do you remember that scandal surrounding that big Protestant church in Portsmouth about eight years ago? They had a preschool there, and a woman and her son were accused of molesting dozens of children. Well, Bob was their attorney, and he won. They didn't serve any jail time at all. He got the case thrown out. I just spoke with him and told him what's going on. He's sitting in his office right now, waiting for your call."

The church in Portsmouth was only about an hour east of Fairview. Luckily, Bob James lived in Fairview, and his office was less than fifteen minutes from the rectory.

I called him on the phone as soon as I hung up with Peter, and forty-five minutes later, Wayne, Adeline, and I were sitting in his waiting room. It was a big place, one of those gorgeous high-rises, all glass, plush furniture, everybody in a suit. The secretary was friendly and efficient and offered us coffee or a soft drink while we waited.

I went into Bob's office, leaving Wayne and Adeline in the waiting room. I told Bob the entire story, beginning with the accusation from five years ago. He listened to every detail, but he didn't take any notes. He said very little, actually. When he finally spoke, he said two things. One, he could help me. Two, he charged five hundred dollars an hour.

I said, "Well, I'm not sure you'll be able to help me. I can't afford five hundred dollars an hour."

"I understand, and I do want this case. Let's do this. I'm going to lower the fee. How about if we say three hundred an hour?" He said that like it was a great deal, which I guess it was compared to five hundred.

"As long as I've got the cash, I'll pay. But when the cash runs out, I'll have to pay you over time. I don't make much as a parish priest." My parents had left me and my brothers some money when they died, but it wasn't nearly enough to cover the cost of this if it went on too long.

"That's fine. As long as something comes in to the firm every month, then we'll be okay. Let me call the diocesan attorney and see if I can get some more details from him. I can't talk directly to the bishop because I represent you, not him, but I can talk to the attorney for the diocese."

I left Bob's office with his assurance that he would take care of everything, and that I should try not to worry—as if that were even an option. I explained everything to Wayne and Adeline on the way home; again, we played the game of *what if*.

They both assured me that they believed me completely, that they knew I wasn't capable of assaulting anyone. They tried their best to make me feel better, and there was a tiny bit of comfort in knowing that I had my two best friends in the entire world who would stand beside me no matter what happened with all of this.

I heard nothing else from anyone for the next week—not the bishop, and not Bob. I tried to go on with business as usual, but every time I met with someone, I wondered if they knew. It felt like I was walking around with a sign on my back that said, 'accused rapist.' Finally, eight days after I left Bob's office, I got a phone call from him.

"Paul, I spoke with the diocesan attorney. Frankly, he doesn't seem to know much more than you or I do at this point. What I do know is that Bishop Robertson is pushing for you to do this psychiatric assessment. I don't like it, and my first instinct is to tell you to refuse. Legally, I don't see any reason why you have to do the assessment, but let's play ball with them. Show them you have nothing to hide, that you're willing to do what it takes to prove you're innocent and make this thing go away. We can compromise with them so that you don't have to go to a residential facility. That way they get what they want, but they get it our way."

The next thing I knew, Bill Russell called to tell me that he'd made appointments for me to see a child psychologist who specialized in child abuse, a general psychologist who took care of people with general psychological disorders, and a psychologist whose specialty was assessments dealing with sexual issues. There was also an appointment with a licensed clinical social worker, although I have no idea why there was a need for that.

All these appointments were spread over about a two-week period. The deal was I would see these people and take a bunch of different psychiatric personality tests and assessments. These were the type of tests that they swear you can't lie your way through because the questions appear quickly and you've got to keep moving from one question to the next. You can't take as much time as you want. I had taken these tests decades ago. All seminarians were required to take them, but I'm sure they had all been updated and reworked over the years.

Over a two-week period, I saw these four people and took the tests. They each submitted a written report to Bill Russell, who then gave the reports to Greg Johns, the priest/clinical psychologist, who was on the diocesan panel. Greg's job was to compile the individual reports into a final submission for the bishop. That process took about two months. I spent a lot of time with Bob James during the two months, mostly going over hypothetical situations, more *what ifs*. So far, Bob's charges weren't too bad, and at least I still had the cash to pay him when the bill came every month.

At the end of June, I got a phone call from Bill Russell, and I went to meet him and Greg Johns at the bishop's office. Greg had compiled all of the results into one massive file—it must have been two inches thick. The results were exactly what I expected them to be: there was nothing in any of the tests that showed any sign that I was capable of sexual abuse. Nothing. I didn't have the personality type of an abuser. Bishop Robertson seemed satisfied. As far as he was concerned, that was all he needed and there was no reason to go further with the investigation.

Just like the last time, I thought it was all over.

CHAPTER TEN

THIRD TIME

Thus, condemnation will never come to those
who are in Christ Jesus, because the law of the Spirit
which gives life in Christ Jesus
has set you free from the law of sin and death.

What the Law could not do because of the weakness
of human nature, God did, sending his own Son
in the same human nature as any sinner to be a sacrifice for sin,
and condemning sin in that human nature.

This was so that the Law's requirements might be fully satisfied in us
as we direct our lives not by our natural inclinations but by the Spirit.

Those who are living by their natural inclinations
have their minds on the things human nature desires;
those who live in the Spirit have their minds on spiritual things.

~ ROMANS 8:1-5

Suddenly it was the end of March 2003, and nine months had gone by without another word from Ryan Williams or his attorney. I had put it out of my mind for the most part, and life had returned to normal.

Then I got a phone call from Bill Russell.

"Did you read yesterday's newspaper? Go get your copy and turn to the classified section. I'll hold on." When I got back to the phone, he told me to turn to the *personals* section and look at the second column, halfway down the page. It was a Monday, early in the season of Lent.

There, in bold print, was an advertisement in the Sunday edition of the *Daily Times:* **Has anybody seen or been in contact with Father Paul Freemont? Does anybody have any stories about Father Paul? Call this number (894) 555-4126.**

"Paul, do you have any idea what this is about?"

"How would I know what it's about? I just saw it. How did you find out about it?"

"A reporter from the *Daily Times* called the chancery this morning and asked me about the ad. Since Bishop Robertson is away, I'm the lucky one who got to take the call. She said that she had called the number in the ad and had spoken with someone, and now she wanted to know what I had to say. I told her that I had no idea what she was talking about, and that I had no comment."

The timing could not have been worse. Bishops are required to make an *ad limina* visit to Rome every five years; they meet with the pope and give a five-year report of what's going on in their diocese. Bishop Robertson had just left the week before to go to Rome, and he wouldn't be back for almost a month.

Bill and I stayed on the phone and tried to discuss strategy, but you can't strategize if you don't even know what game you're playing. Bill and I agreed that it wasn't necessary to contact the bishop at that point; we didn't even know for sure who placed the ad and what they were trying to find out. Neither of us wanted to call the number to find out who would answer, and looking back, I'm not sure why. The only choice was to wait.

The same ad ran for three more Sundays in a row, the last one on April thirteenth, Palm Sunday. In the four weeks that the ad ran, no one contacted me or anyone in the diocesan offices, other than the reporter who spoke with Bill Russell the day after the first ad. I was waiting for the unimaginable, terrified, wondering what this all meant and what would happen next. Obviously, I thought that this must be Ryan Williams again.

Bishop Robertson returned from Rome on Tuesday, April twenty-second, thirty days after the first newspaper ad.

At precisely five o'clock on Friday the twenty-fifth, my office phone rang. Adeline had just left, so I answered it myself.

"Paul! It's Norma. How are you? I won't keep you. I know you're busy. The bishop would like for you to come see him in his office on Monday morning at nine o'clock."

"Norma, what's going on? This is about those personal ads in the paper, isn't it? I've been trying to figure this thing out for the past month. Surely someone at the chancery knows something."

"Honey, I wish I knew. I need to run. It's past five o'clock and the traffic will be awful. You have a wonderful weekend. See you Monday morning." She hung up. And that was it, a weekend of waiting and worrying.

Mondays were usually my day off. After a weekend of presiding over five liturgies, hospital visits, throw in a baptism and sometimes a wedding, by Monday I was exhausted. This Monday was different. I was antsy, anxious, running on caffeine after a weekend of no sleep. I left early to be sure that I could get a parking spot near the chancery. I parked two blocks away, and the spring air was just cool enough to give me a chill when the breeze touched my sweaty brow.

It was just past eight-thirty when I walked into the chancery and took the stairs to the bishop's office on the second floor. Norma was already at her desk, and she greeted me with her usual hugs and southern charm.

"It's so good to see you! Can I get you some coffee? Did you have breakfast yet, 'cause I brought muffins this morning!"

I turned down the coffee and muffin; I asked for a Diet Coke instead. I'd never learned to tolerate coffee, so Diet Coke was my caffeine of choice.

At five minutes until nine, Bishop Robertson opened his office door and told me to come in, and he shut the door behind us. You could feel the tension in the air, thick and miserable. The look on his face told me that something horrible had happened.

"Paul, let's get right to the point. This Ryan Williams thing has gotten out of hand. This is the third time, and he has a new lawyer."

"I knew it! That was Williams who ran those newspaper ads before Easter! Why is he doing this again? I assume you know more than just *it's gotten out of hand, and he has a new lawyer.*"

"It's different this time. He has people, students from St. Joseph, that are backing him up. It's bad, Paul, and I'm not sure it won't get worse pretty soon. I'm giving you one week to get your things together, then you'll be on leave until we can sort this thing out. Maybe you can take a little trip, go somewhere and relax for a while. I think you should make an announcement at all of the liturgies this weekend."

"What in the hell are you talking about? What people? You're putting me on leave? Bishop, have you lost your mind?" I slammed both of my hands on his desk as I stood up and leaned over to the point where our faces were uncomfortably close. He actually seemed to shrink back in his chair as if he thought it was me who had lost my mind.

"Paul, sit. You need to calm down. So far, two more have contacted me, both former students of yours at St. Joseph. Williams' attorney says others will come forward soon."

"Come forward with what? Who? I didn't do anything! Nothing happened at St. Joseph! We've been through this. Williams had a drug problem back then, and it sounds like he still does! Bishop, you have to remember—Williams told you almost six years ago that the other student, David Baxter, would back up his story. Then David Baxter said none of it ever happened. I've had psych assessments that showed you I'm innocent! You've seen the reports."

"Paul . . ."

"How much money does he want?" That's all I could come up with that even began to make sense. It had to be about money.

"Same as before, a million. David Baxter has changed his story and someone else named Wayne Michaels says he has information about something you did, too. Michaels was a student at St. Joseph, but a few years before Williams and Baxter. I don't think Michaels even knew the other two until now."

The room suddenly started to spin, my ears were ringing, I couldn't breathe. I thought I might pass out. The bishop was talking, but I couldn't hear him.

Wayne Michaels.

One of my best friends.

CHAPTER ELEVEN

FIRST TO LEAVE

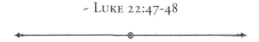

While he was still speaking a crowd approached,
and in front was one of the Twelve, a man named Judas.
He went up to Jesus to kiss Him.

Jesus said to him,
"Judas, are you betraying the Son of Man with a kiss?"

~ Luke 22:47-48

Slowly, I tuned back in to the bishop's words.

"Williams' attorney says there are more, but I don't know how many more there are. You need to say something this weekend at liturgy. It's better for people to hear it from you than to read this stuff in the newspaper. You need to prepare a statement to read this weekend. I'd like to see it first, but I think you should read it at each one of the liturgies.

You have a week to wrap up whatever you need to, but you're on leave a week from today."

The fog was starting to lift, and the words were beginning to make sense. I heard what he was saying. I just couldn't wrap my brain around what he was telling me.

"For how long? I can't just *go on leave*. I have a parish to take care of. I have weddings, baptisms, there's so much."

"No. Starting a week from today, you're not to serve as pastor in any capacity at St. Edward until I tell you otherwise. I think it'll be best if you don't go to the church at all. It'll be easier that way, less confusing for everyone. *No pastoral duties anywhere, Paul.* No liturgy, no baptisms, no weddings. Nothing."

"This is bullshit! I need to call my attorney."

"You don't need your attorney. Let's keep this simple. We can figure this out. No need to get any more attorneys involved unless we have to. Paul, just go back to the rectory, pour yourself a drink, try to calm down. Maybe go for a walk, then get a good night's sleep. Tomorrow you can work on your statement. I'd like to have it by Wednesday to approve what you're going to say. Keep it simple, don't tell too much."

"Don't tell too much? What in the hell does that mean? I don't even know what's going on! How can I tell too much when I don't know a damn thing? I don't even know how long I'll be on leave. Can you at least tell me that?" The question hung in the air, unanswered.

The bishop nodded at the door. "Go home, Paul."

I don't remember the walk to my car or the drive home. I didn't go for a walk, and I didn't sleep. I just kept playing everything over and over in my mind. None of it was adding up. Without thinking, I reached for my phone to call Wayne, but I obviously couldn't call him anymore. I called Adeline instead. She met me at the house and tried to make me eat, but I couldn't. Thank God for her. I'm not sure how I would have survived without her support. Things were no clearer in the morning. If anything, I was more confused than I was yesterday. When Ryan Williams first accused me six years prior of assaulting him in the 1970s, he had told the bishop that David Baxter would back him up. But Baxter said that it never happened. He called Williams a druggie and said that Williams imagined the whole thing.

Why would David Baxter change his story? I had seen Baxter a few months ago, before all of this ugliness resurfaced. He and his wife happened to be in Fairview, and they came to the eleven o'clock Mass at St. Edward. I hadn't seen David Baxter in years, but when he came up to me after Mass, I knew exactly who he was. He was always such a nice kid. He gave me the biggest hug. I mean, I thought I was going to pop.

We talked for at least twenty minutes. "It was just so good to hear you preach again," he said, and he seemed genuinely happy to see me. He told me about his family, and we talked about the old days at St. Joseph. I had to cut our talk short because I had to leave for an appointment with a couple who were planning their wedding. He hugged me again before he left and told me not to be a stranger. He even gave me his phone number and told me to call him if I was ever in Bristol, where he lived. And yet, a few months later, he was accusing me of something that the bishop said was *bad*, no details, just *bad*.

The hardest part to come to terms with was hearing that Wayne, my *friend,* was part of this accusation against me. Less than a year ago, when Ryan Williams had resurfaced for the second time, Wayne had been the first person I called. It had been embarrassing, the whole ugly thing. I had known that Wayne would understand because he had been a student at St. Joseph, and that he wouldn't judge me because he was my friend.

Now Wayne was accusing me.

Accusing me of what?

He had been the voice of reason when I panicked.

He had told me everything would be fine.

I was terrified, and he had helped me calm down.

He had gone with me to meet my attorney.

He had assured me that it would blow over.

I had trusted him.

Wayne had never known Ryan Williams or David Baxter; he had graduated before they arrived at St. Joseph. What was the connection? There had to be a connection, but I couldn't come up with it.

And there might be others, according to the bishop. Others? How could there be others? I had done *nothing* wrong.

I had to put that out of my mind. I needed to focus on writing the statement that I would read at the liturgies during the upcoming weekend. There were five liturgies, one on Saturday evening and four on Sunday. Whatever I wrote, I would have to read *five* times, but I knew I could never do that. The thought of reading it once was tearing me apart, and I hadn't even begun to write it. I could get through Saturday night if I had to, but I knew that there was no way I could stand up in front of hundreds of people and read it four more times on Sunday. Besides, by Sunday morning, the rumor mill would have spread the word for me.

I decided to call Lewis Waller, a retired priest who helped around the diocese when a priest went on vacation or got sick. I told Lewis as little as I could, just enough to get him to agree to handle the four Sunday liturgies, then I got to work on the statement that I would read on Saturday.

I waited until the very end of liturgy, then I walked to the podium, reached through the opening in the side of my alb, the white tunic that covered my street clothes, and pulled the paper from my pocket.

"Good evening to you all. We seem to have a full house, don't we? For those of you who are visiting us here at St. Edward, welcome. Your presence blesses my fellow Edwardians and me. I ask that you all indulge me for the next few minutes, as I have something very serious and very difficult to say to you this evening. I've prepared something that I'd like to read to you now."

That should have been a red flag that something was wrong to anyone who was paying attention. I never used notes or read prepared statements when standing at a podium. I was in constant motion when I spoke, walking around the circular worship space to be sure that parishioners in each section felt included.

That was the very moment when I looked up and saw him out of the corner of my eye. Wayne. He was sitting across from me, in the top row of the section behind the choir.

He was alone, but he always came to Mass alone since his divorce. Wayne showed no emotion at all in his face; he was just sitting there, hunched over with his hands on his knees and staring at me, as if waiting to hear what I had to say so that he could get up and leave. I gripped the podium until my knuckles were white and tried to hide the pain shooting through me, like a knife was being plunged into my gut and twisted over and over. I wondered if I might pass out. I wished I would.

"Five days ago, on Monday, I had a meeting with Bishop Robertson. He called me to his office to have a very difficult conversation with me, and I must share that with you all tonight. While I cannot disclose all of the details of our conversation, I can tell you that there have been some serious accusations of impropriety made against me. These accusations stem from my time at St. Joseph Seminary in Rutherford County, where I served as principal over twenty years ago.

"I can assure you that these accusations are completely false; I am innocent of any impropriety. I am certain that my innocence will be proven soon. However, accusations of improper behavior among clergy must be taken very seriously, and Bishop Robertson is following the proper protocol to

investigate this to the fullest extent. There is an investigative team in place that will thoroughly look into these accusations.

"Once again, I assure all of you that I am innocent of any impropriety. In the meantime, I am taking a leave of absence as your pastor, beginning immediately after this liturgy. Father Lewis Waller will preside over to-morrow's liturgies, and the bishop will assign an interim pastor to serve the parish until I return, which I expect will be very soon. I ask that you pray for me, as I will for you. I will see you all again when the diocese finishes with the investigation. God Bless you all."

I looked up to see Wayne walking toward the door. All I could think of was that *Judas was the first to leave.*

CHAPTER TWELVE

THE DAILY TIMES

If the world hates you, you must realize
that it hated me before it hated you.

If you belonged to the world, the world would love you as its own;
but because you do not belong to the world, because my choice of you
has drawn you out of the world, that is why the world hates you.

Remember the words I said to you: A servant is not greater
than his master. If they persecuted me, they will persecute you too;
if they kept my word, they will keep yours as well.

~ JOHN 15:18-20

STUDENTS AT DEFUNCT CATHOLIC BOYS SCHOOL
ACCUSE PRIEST OF ABUSE
~ by Linda Albert, Daily Times staff writer

Like so many of his peers at St. Joseph Seminary in Rutherford County, Ryan Williams, a student there in the mid-1970s, wanted to be a priest. And, like so many of those peers, Williams changed his mind.

St. Joseph Seminary opened in 1960 and closed its doors in 1978 after enrollment had dropped to the point where the late Bishop Theodore Saunders, then bishop of the Catholic Diocese of Fairview, no longer saw it as a financially viable operation.

At the time of its closing, the principal was Father Paul Freemont, now pastor of St. Edward Catholic Church in Springfield. Father Paul, as he was known to the students then and is known to the parishioners now, brought new life to the seminary when he arrived in 1968. His relaxed, progressive demeanor is remembered by many of his former students as liberating. The young priest, still in his twenties when he arrived at St. Joseph, could have easily been mistaken for one of the students.

While many former students remember Father Paul as a gifted principal, teacher, and spiritual advisor, others remember him quite differently. Ryan Williams is one of those students.

In July 1997, Williams contacted Bishop Thomas Robertson, the current bishop of the Diocese of Fairview, with accusations that he had been sexually abused by as a student at St. Joseph over twenty years ago. According to Williams, Bishop Robertson performed a cursory internal investigation and brushed his accusations aside. Williams, traumatized, he says, by having his accusations so easily dismissed by Bishop Robertson, did nothing to further pursue this for almost five years. Williams has said that he could not afford legal representation at that time, and did not know what, if any, recourse he had.

Last April, almost exactly twelve months ago, Williams again contacted Bishop Robertson, this time through an attorney. He asked the bishop to reopen the investigations into the allegations that Freemont had sexually abused him in the 1970s when he was a student at St. Joseph Seminary. According to Williams, Bishop Robertson notified his attorney, after a two-month period, that the matter had once again been fully investigated by the diocese, and that no action was to be taken against Freemont. The bishop's investigative team had found Williams' accusations to be lacking in credibility, according to Williams. Father Freemont has continued in his role as pastor at St. Edward Catholic Church throughout that investigation.

Last month, Williams decided that he could no longer accept the answers he was given by Bishop Robertson and the Diocese of Fairview, so he ran a series of advertisements in the Daily Times encouraging anyone with information about Father Paul Freemont to contact him. The response to those advertisements may be just what Williams needs to make Bishop Robertson take notice.

According to Williams, five former St. Joseph students have contacted him and have come forward to make their own claims of sexual abuse against Father Paul Freemont. One former faculty member has also come forward with information that he claims will substantiate the allegations made by those former students.

The Daily Times has spoken with another former St. Joseph student who has reported that Father Paul Freemont has been removed as pastor of St. Edward. According to this source, who wishes to remain anonymous and who was present at a service held last night at St. Edward, Father Freemont read a prepared statement at the end of the service informing the parishioners that Bishop Robertson has placed him on an immediate leave of absence.

We will continue to report updates as they become available.

Once the article ran in the *Daily Times,* which was the day after I announced I was being placed on leave, the whole situation took on a life of its own. Looking back, I think that Bishop Robertson and I were both incredibly naïve. I don't think either one of us imagined that this thing would go beyond the diocesan investigation, much less become the topic of local news. Robertson said he would handle it, and that was his plan. He had handled it twice before, so I assumed he would again.

Once I calmed down, I expected this would all go away, just like it had the past two times. I should have known this time would be different when I got the phone call from him on Tuesday, two days after the article.

"Paul, this thing with Ryan Williams is just getting to be too much. Newspaper reporters keep calling me. Two different television reporters were waiting for me when I got out of my car this morning at the chancery; they even had their cameras pointed at me! I can't spend all of my time trying to figure this out. This is the third time in six years that this has come up. Are you sure there isn't something you're not telling me? Maybe something you forgot about, but now you remember?"

"No! There is not anything I *forgot* to tell you! I can't believe you would even say that to me. You've known me for years, for decades. Do you really think I'm capable of sexually abusing teenage boys?"

"I know, I know. But I had to ask. Listen, I'm going to turn this over to Carl Walters. He has a lot more time than I do, and he'll do a good job of looking into all of this. He's been offering to help with this mess, and I think that's the right thing to do. I'll have him call you when he knows more about what's going on."

"You can't do that! Walters hates me. He's pompous and arrogant. He'll do anything he can to make this harder on me than it already is."

Carl Walters was taking his job as the new auxiliary bishop very seriously. Bishop Robertson's retirement was fast approaching, and Walters was eager to garner as much control of the diocese as he could while Robertson slowed down.

Walters and I had known each other for years, and we had never gotten along. Maybe it was a personality conflict, but neither one of us could stand to be in the same room as the other.

"Paul, that's my decision. Carl will look into everything. He'll let me know what he finds out, and I'll decide what we need to do. He'll call you when he needs to talk to you."

And that was it. The phone line was dead.

CHAPTER THIRTEEN

THE ACCUSERS

When Jesus was at dinner in his house, a number of tax collectors
and sinners were also sitting at table with Jesus and his disciples;
for there were many of them among his followers.

When the scribes of the Pharisee party saw him eating with sinners
and tax collectors, they said to his disciples,
'Why does he eat with tax collectors and sinners?'

When Jesus heard this he said to them,
'It is not the healthy who need the doctor, but the sick.
I came to call not the upright, but sinners.'

~ MARK 2:15-17

For the next month, Walters met with or spoke to each of the accusers—five former students in addition to Williams, and one former faculty member.

Ryan Williams' story kept changing, or actually, it kept growing. Suddenly Williams remembered even more details. He admitted that he was an addict but said I was the reason for his drug addiction because I had given him drugs at St. Joseph. He claimed he had never used drugs until he met me. I had allegedly supplied him with little yellow pills to keep him stoned so that I could molest him. He said that was the reason I *pretended* not to notice his drug use when he was a student.

Williams claimed that he earned money during his summers at St. Joseph by going along with the abuse, not by painting the dorms and working on the property. According to the new story, I had turned him into a drug addict so that I could control him and use him for sex. The abuse, he said, happened weekly, sometimes more often, and that it went much deeper than the theater stage or the ménage à trois with David Baxter.

As much as Walters disliked me, even he acknowledged that Williams seemed confused and inconsistent when they met to discuss the accusations. Walters said that Williams' attorney looked surprised at some of the additional details that came out in the meeting.

Next was David Baxter, who ended up recanting his story when Bishop Walters spoke with him. Baxter told the bishop that he couldn't meet in person but would be happy to speak on the phone since what he had to say would be quick.

Baxter told the bishop that Williams had called him around the time that all the newspaper ads were running. Williams insisted to Baxter that I had molested him when they were students at St. Joseph. Baxter said he felt sorry for Williams, and that he began to wonder if maybe Williams was telling the truth. He questioned himself; he had been a teenager at the time and maybe he hadn't realized what was going on.

Williams told Baxter that he needed money, the diocese would pay him, and no one was getting hurt because justice was being served. He asked Baxter to call Bishop Robertson and back up his story, so that's what Baxter did.

Once the article went to print, Baxter knew he had made a mistake, and he didn't want to be involved anymore. He admitted to Bishop Walters that he had never witnessed me doing anything sexual with a student. He told Walters to never contact him again.

Lane Simon was the third. He came to St. Joseph about three years after I arrived. Simon was a nice kid, goofy, very small for his age. He played soccer. Of course, he was always running around with the jock crowd. I was his spiritual advisor, so we spent a good bit of time together. What I remember most about him is how you could be walking down the hallway, and suddenly someone would jump up on your back, and it was Simon. That was the type of stuff he did. He was also one of the kids who always begged to go to the middle schools to help us recruit students to St. Joseph.

When Simon spoke with Walters, he said he had been in my office one day during his sophomore year, and I got up from my chair and started hugging him and told him I *needed* him. He also told Walters that I always made them take off their clothes and go streaking when we went on the beach retreats, and that I told them they could only go swimming in the pool at St. Joseph if they did so in the nude. Yet, he never told a soul, and he spent four years there and graduated.

Fourth was Travis Dodson. Not a theater kid or a jock—he was part of the *everybody else* crowd. Dodson told Walters that I had made him come to my room at least once a week, sometimes more, so I could give him back rubs.

He said it was creepy; he hated it, but he didn't think he had a choice because I was the principal. Dodson said I would rub lotion all over his back, and that I always rubbed too low. He said he didn't say anything because he was ashamed; even though he hated it, he would get aroused every time.

Dodson's story was partially true. I did call him into my room for back rubs every few days, but it was because his mother insisted. She had sent a couple of bottles of lotion to me, with instructions that it must be rubbed on his back at least every three days. She said he was very fragile. Those were her words, and she said this would help his muscles.

I thought she was a little off, but she was adamant that I needed to do this since she wasn't there to do it herself. Since there was no doctor or nurse on staff to apply the lotion, it seemed like I had no choice but to go along with her and do it myself. As weird as I thought it was, I didn't see it as sexual. In my mind, I was indulging an over-protective, maybe possessive, mother.

Wayne's story involved another student, Josh Davis; they were the last of the six students who met with Walters. Wayne's accusation was the hardest one for me to hear, even harder than the accusations by Ryan Williams. Although Williams' accusations were the most damning, I knew that he had completely fabricated his story, and I felt certain the truth would eventually come out.

The problem with Wayne's story was that it was one hundred per-cent true. I was guilty of everything Wayne and Davis accused me of. Although I hadn't thought of that story in years, once it came up again, I remembered it like it was yesterday.

Wayne and Davis were best friends at St. Joseph. They were insep-arable then, and they had remained friends for years after they grad-uated. Both were athletic and very competitive; they were part of the *jock* crowd. When Wayne and Josh were at St. Joseph, they were both standout soccer players.

One day in the early spring, just before soccer season, their coach, Thomas Alderman, came to my office and told me that he needed some equipment from the sporting goods store in Fairview. He wanted me to give him a blank check so he could go shopping. Back in the 1970s, that's how it worked at a small, private school; you went to the store, picked out what you needed, and paid with a check. There was no overnight delivery, and the schools didn't use credit cards back then.

I had put Alderman on a tight budget because he had a bad habit of spending way too much money on things that the kids didn't need. There was no way I was going to give him a blank check and turn him loose in a sporting goods store. The soccer team had more than enough fancy sweatsuits thanks to the last time I had given Alderman a blank check.

I told him that I was going to Fairview the next day after school, so he could give me a list and I'd pick up what he needed. He pointed out that I knew nothing about sporting equipment, which was true, so he suggested that I take Wayne Michaels and Josh Davis, two seniors on the team, because they'd know exactly what to get.

The next day, after classes, the three of us drove to Fairview. The drive there was uneventful, but on the drive back, the two of them began to argue almost as soon as we got in the car. At first, they seemed to be having fun, but after a few minutes I realized it was serious and they were truly getting angry. That's when I started to pay attention to their conversation. They were arguing about their penises.

We had filled the trunk of my 1965 Pontiac Bonneville with the things on Alderman's list, and on that list were a bunch of jockstraps in a variety of different sizes. Wayne was in the front seat and Josh was in the back. Josh was the one who started the whole ridiculous argument.

"Hey, Wayne, Coach got a couple of those jock straps in a size small. Those are for you, man."

Wayne seemed to laugh it off. "No, man, those are yours. The extra-large is for me. Your wanker needs an extra small, if they even make 'em in that size."

Josh leaned over the front seat. "Yeah, you wish. Mine's a lot bigger than yours, man. You're a putz."

"Tighten up, Joshie, you must be stoned. Everybody on the team knows how little yours is. Why do you think they laugh at you in the shower?"

Suddenly Josh slammed the palms of both of his hands into the back of Wayne's seat. I almost ran the car off of the road; I'd had enough.

"You two need to calm down right now! I will NOT listen to this for another forty-five minutes, and I won't wreck my car because you don't know how to act. I don't care what you talk about, or if you shut your mouths for the rest of the ride back, but no more of this! When we get back to the school, you can take your penises out of your pants and compare if you want to, but you're done having this conversation in my car."

The rest of the ride was completely silent, but the tension in the air was almost worse than the arguing. When we got back to the school, they unloaded the car without speaking a word to each other, took everything to the gym, and then, I assume, they went to their dorm. I have no idea what happened after that. And now, over thirty years later, they say that this was sexual abuse.

They told Bishop Walters that they were traumatized, and from that moment on they were afraid of what I would say or do to them. But they both admitted I never said or did anything after that day to cause them to be concerned.

They were eighteen; I was twenty-nine. It was a different time. I'd never say that type of thing to anyone now, especially knowing how easy it is for words to be twisted. Looking back, I wish I'd have just let them fight it out in the car. I wish I'd have never said a word, but I was incredibly naïve and young. I had no idea that one sentence would come back to haunt me decades later.

When Walters spoke with Wayne Michaels and Josh Davis, they both told the same story, which was almost exactly as I remembered it. They told the truth about what happened that day, but somehow, thirty years later, that conversation in the car turned into sex abuse.

Wayne had been one of my best friends for over a decade, and now this. It made no sense. He had never mentioned it to me in all of those years. I hadn't seen Josh Davis since he graduated, but now and then Wayne would tell me that he had spoken to Josh on the phone or had seen him and that Josh said to tell me *hello*. Why would they suddenly decide that the conversation all those years ago had traumatized them?

When I found out who the last accuser was, the faculty member, it all started to make sense.

CHAPTER FOURTEEN

THE COACH

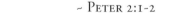

As there were false prophets in the past history of our people,
so you too will have your false teachers, who will insinuate their
own disruptive views and, by disowning the Lord who bought
them freedom, will bring upon themselves speedy destruction.

Many will copy their debauched behaviour, and the Way
of Truth will be brought into disrepute on their account.

~ Peter 2:1-2

The final accusation came from Thomas Alderman, the soccer coach
at St. Joseph. Alderman had been a part-time staff member at St. Joseph
in 1969 and 1970; he only lasted there a couple of years. I had hired
him out of desperation. We had needed a soccer coach and were having
a hard time finding someone willing to work part-time at a remote all-
boys school.

Alderman seemed like the perfect fit. He worked full-time for the diocese; he didn't mind the drive to St. Joseph in the afternoon, and he had played soccer in high school and college. And he was the only person who applied for the job.

Alderman's only student interaction was with the jocks, and Josh Davis was what we called a *super jock* back then. Davis was Alderman's golden boy; he rarely missed a goal and was a starter in every game.

Where Josh Davis was a coach's dream, Thomas Alderman was a principal's nightmare. He spent the school's money on frivolous things, and he never got permission first. The kids on the soccer team were almost always late to evening prayer because Alderman kept them late for practice. I would tell him that he needed to end practice on time, he'd agree, then he'd keep them late again. He made his own rules. Those things were annoying, but I could deal with them.

I had to fire Alderman for a much more serious reason.

When Alderman applied for the coaching job, I didn't take time to verify any of his information. I was young and inexperienced, and it seemed unnecessary. He worked for the diocese already, and I assumed that they had vetted him prior to hiring him years before. I found out I was wrong almost two years after he took the job as a soccer coach.

St. Joseph was accredited by the National Association of Catholic Schools, and in order to keep the accreditation, they required us to submit documentation every three years with information about our faculty and staff, coaches included. The NACS wanted to know the educational level of each person, what they were certified to teach, that type of thing.

Unfortunately for Alderman, his second year was a re-accreditation year. When I pulled Alderman's file to get his information, I noticed that his employment application stated he had a master's degree in education. However, the name of the university was missing, and I needed that for the NACS paperwork.

I phoned the diocesan human resource office to get the information; they, too, were missing the name of the university where he got his master's degree. Next, I called Alderman into my office and asked him to tell me the name of the school where he got his master's degree. I didn't care for him, but I never thought for even a minute that he had lied on his employment application. I thought it was simply an oversight.

He flew into a rage. He jumped up from his chair, face blood-red, and started screaming like a maniac.

"Why in the hell are you looking in my file? I told you what you need to know on the application. My life is none of your business. You think you know so much, you with your little drama boys. Why don't you go back to them and leave me the hell alone!"

Alderman wasn't the most pleasant person to be around, but even for him, this was extreme.

"Thomas, what are you even talking about? All I want is the name of the school where you got your master's degree. I need it for the accreditation paperwork. Clearly, there's something going on here that I don't know about. Is there something you'd like to explain?"

"St. George University." He slammed the door as he walked out. At least now I knew the name of the school, but something just didn't feel right. Curiosity got the best of me, and I decided to make a few phone calls to see what I could find out. Today there are so many privacy laws that it's hard to get anyone to tell you anything, but back then it was easier.

I picked up my office phone, dialed 555-1212, the phone number for directory assistance back then, and got the number for the Office of Graduate Studies at St. George University in Maryland.

"Hello, Office of Graduate Studies. This is Gloria, may I help you?"

"Gloria, my name is Father Paul Freemont. I'm calling from St. Joseph Seminary School in Virginia. I was hoping you could help me."

"I'll try, Father. I just love Virginia. My sister and her husband used to live there years ago. I drove down to visit a few times. What is it you need help with?"

"I'm trying to surprise one of our teachers. He's receiving an award from the diocese, the Outstanding Educator of the Year. It's quite an honor. We wanted to include some of his accomplishments during the award ceremony. I know that he received his master's degree in education from St. George several years ago, but I'm not certain of the exact year. Is there any way that you could find that out for me?" I lied, but I couldn't see any other way to find out what was going on with Alderman.

"Oh Father, how nice of you. I love surprises! I'm sure he'll be so thrilled. What an honor! It might take me a little while to go through the boxes and find his information. The files that go back more than two years are in the storage room. Is it okay if I call you back? I'm sure I can find it and call you back before the end of the day."

"Gloria, my dear, that would be wonderful!" I gave her my phone number and spent the next few hours in my office waiting for her to call me back with the answer to Alderman's big mystery.

When Gloria called me back, the tone in her voice had changed. Gone was the cheerful, bubbly Gloria that I'd spoken with a few hours ago. This Gloria was hesitant and guarded with her words. "Father, this is Gloria from St. George. I'm very sorry, but I don't think I'll be able to help you."

"You didn't find his file?" So that was it. He'd lied about going to St. George.

"No, Father, I found his file. There are just some things . . ." Her voice trailed off, then silence.

"Gloria? Are you still there?"

"Yes, Father. I'm here. I just don't think I can help you."

"I don't understand. I just need to know the year he graduated. I want Thomas' award ceremony to be perfect."

"Oh, Father, I just, well, I just don't know how to say this." She was whispering and sounded like her throat may close up at any second. I could barely hear her. "He didn't graduate."

"What? Did you say that he didn't graduate? Are you sure?"

"Yes, Father, I'm sure." I knew from the tone of embarrassment in her voice that there was more. After a brief hesitation, she blurted out, "Father, he was asked to leave St. George. That's why he never graduated."

"What do you mean by *he was asked to leave?*"

"Oh, Father, I just don't know if I can tell you this. I don't think it's appropriate."

"Tell me what?"

"There were some undergraduate students, Father, some girls. He was a teaching assistant. The girls said he offered to give them better grades for . . . Well, you know, Father. I don't think I can say any more. Father, I'm so sorry."

"Oh, no Gloria, please don't apologize. You've been so helpful. You are a true asset to St. George University. Please don't give this another thought. I'm so sorry if I've done anything to upset you, dear."

At least now I understood why Alderman exploded when I asked him about his master's degree. There was no question about what I needed to do. Alderman needed to leave St. Joseph, and the diocese needed to know about all of this.

Once again, I called Alderman and told him to come into my office. When I told him that I had spoken to someone at St. George, he exploded.

"You son of a bitch! I told you to stick with your drama boys and stay out of my business." He looked like a raging bull, ready to charge. I wondered if he might explode right there in front of me.

"Would you like to explain?" I asked as calmly as I could. As much as I disliked him, he deserved a chance to tell his side.

"I'll explain. Yeah, I'll explain that you can KISS MY ASS! How's that for an explanation? KISS MY ASS!"

That was enough. I had no choice but to tell him to leave the campus immediately. We didn't have any type of security at the school, and I never stopped to think about what I would have done if he had refused to leave.

Luckily, he walked out, but this time he didn't slam the door when he left. As he walked out, he looked back through the open door, smiling as if there were something he dared not say.

"I won't forget this," he said in a voice so flat and eerily calm that I felt a shiver up my spine.

CHAPTER FIFTEEN

THE DECISION

He himself made human beings in the beginning,
and then left them free to make their own decisions.

If you choose, you will keep the commandments
and so be faithful to his will.

He has set fire and water before you;
put out your hand to whichever you prefer.

A human being has life and death before him;
whichever he prefers will be given him.

~ SIRACH 15:14-17

Six weeks after Bishop Robertson placed me on leave, I was back in his office to hear the verdict. There was a tremendous feeling of relief. I was certain that Bishop Walters' report to Robertson would prove that I had done nothing wrong.

"Paul, it's good to see you. I hope that you've used these past six weeks for prayer and reflection. It's been a difficult time, I'm sure. I think that this situation has been eye opening for both of us."

I nodded, but I wanted him to get to the point. "Thank you, Bishop. I'd just like . . ."

With that, his hand shot up, palm out, fingers spread wide, as if to tell me to stop. I knew that hand motion all too well. Robertson used it often, typically when he was annoyed or bored. If Bishop Robertson presided at Mass, you were certain to see the hand shoot up if he felt like the choir had gone on for too long.

"I don't think we need to rehash all of this. Bishop Walters has given me his report, and I've made my decision. I know that you and Walters don't always see eye-to-eye, but he was thorough in his report. He spoke with the seven of them. Williams is the only one who accused you of what I would consider sexual assault, and frankly, his story doesn't add up—too many changes. Baxter said he agreed to go along with Williams, but he didn't witness anything . . ."

"Yes, just like he said the first time!" I barely got the words out before the hand shot up again.

"Simon's story is hard to prove either way, in my opinion. You've always been a hugger. Everyone knows that. Maybe you hugged a little too much, I don't know. And that streaking thing, you never should have allowed that to happen. But it was a long time ago, and maybe Simon's memory is a little off on that. It could have been his idea, who knows.

"I will admit that the Dodson thing sounds a little odd. But again, it doesn't sound like you actually *did* anything. Poor judgment once again, but there's nothing we can do about that now."

Robertson continued, "This thing with Wayne Michaels and Josh Davis and that teacher, Alderman, well, I can't get a good grip on that . . ."

"How does Alderman . . .?" The hand stopped me again.

"Alderman told Bishop Walters that Michaels and Davis came to him the day you told them to take their penises out of their pants. He said that they were very upset, and they didn't know who else to tell."

"But, Bishop, that's not exactly how it happened!" No hand this time.

"Alderman also said that Simon complained to him at practice one day that you were getting a little too friendly with him, and that he told Simon just to keep his distance from you."

I still couldn't understand why none of this came up all those years ago.

"Paul, none of that matters now. I'm putting an end to this once and for all. You said some stupid things a long time ago, okay? You know better now. The other stuff with Williams, well, there isn't enough proof for me to do anything. Just go back to St. Edward and, please Paul, don't do anything to bring this back up."

Don't do anything to bring this back up? What had I done to bring it up in the first place?

"Yes, Bishop, thank you." Once again, the hand came up, this time with the palm open toward the door; his way of letting me know it was time to leave.

The next seven weeks were completely normal. I was back at St. Edward doing what I loved, serving the parish. That all ended one morning during the first week of August when Adeline buzzed the intercom on my office phone to tell me that the bishop's office was calling. When I answered, the bishop himself was on the other end, not Norma. I knew this couldn't be good.

"Paul, I need you to come to the chancery this afternoon around two o'clock." Then he hung up. Even for him, that was abrupt.

The next few hours crept by at a painfully slow pace, but finally it was time to drive to the meeting with the bishop. I arrived at the chancery and walked upstairs to Robertson's office. Norma wasn't at her desk. Robertson's door was open, and he motioned for me to come in.

"Close the door, Paul. I got a phone call early this morning from Cardinal Santana." I'd never met Santana, but he had a reputation as a hardass. His office was in Biltmore, Maryland, about three hours north of Fairview. I couldn't imagine what this had to do with me.

"We have a problem. Actually, there's something I didn't tell you the last time you were here. Carl Walters didn't actually think you were innocent, and he didn't want me to reinstate you after his investigation. He and I disagreed about that, but I told him that I was the bishop, and the decision was mine. I had no idea he'd actually go over my head . . ."

"Go over . . ." The hand went up. So that's why Santana called Robertson. I wasn't surprised that Walters had something to do with this.

"Bishop Walters went to the cardinal. My hands are tied. I have no choice. I'm sorry. Cardinal Santana has insisted that we go deeper with this. He's not happy with the way I handled it. He wants it turned over to the Rutherford County Sheriff's Department. Let them sort this whole thing out. You know I'm retiring in a few months. It's better for the sheriff's office to clean this thing up."

"Clean this thing up! The sheriff's department? What does that mean to me? Am I going to be arrested? I didn't do anything!"

"This is out of my hands. And there's more. Bishop Walters contacted the members of the Diocesan Clergy Investigative Panel." I frowned. DCIP is a six-member panel of laypersons whose job is to investigate allegations of impropriety by clergy, sexual abuse included.

He continued, "Four of the six members of the panel emailed me today with their resignations. They said they were entitled to investigate this on their own, and I had denied them that right. Their position is that the panel had been put in place for situations just like this, and they're all furious that I kept it from them. So, now I have to deal with that. Why don't you go back to your office? You should probably call your attorney. Or maybe take the day off. Think about what you want to do."

"Wait, you're not removing me? You've turned me over to the sheriff's office, you've basically accused me of sexually abusing those boys, but you're telling me to go back to the parish office and go about my business?"

There was no sweating, no ears ringing, no fear this time. My thinking was perfectly clear, and I knew that from that point forward, this was all up to me.

I left the bishop's office and drove straight to see Bob James, my attorney. I called Adeline to tell her what had happened and to let her know that I'd be out for the rest of the day.

When I arrived, Bob's secretary said he was in a meeting, but I could wait if I wanted to. After about forty-five minutes of reading the latest copy of *Law Review Monthly*, Bob walked out of his office with a man about my age, shook his hand as he left, and told me to come in and have a seat.

I told Bob about my meeting with the bishop. He said he'd make a phone call to the sheriff's office in the morning and see what was going on. He promised to call me as soon as he knew more.

Bob called the next morning, but with no answers. The deputy at the sheriff's office took his name and told him that someone from their office would be in touch. They hadn't even opened an investigation, so there were no charges being filed by the district attorney at this point. Bob felt certain that this would go away on its own after the sheriff investigated.

Three days later, there was another article in the *Daily Times*.

CATHOLIC BISHOP TAKES BAD TO WORSE
- by Hal Walberg, Daily Times staff writer

This week the Catholic Diocese of Fairview showed a perfect example of how easily a situation can spiral out of control when not handled properly.

Bishop Thomas Robertson, bishop of the Diocese of Fairview, has often been quoted in various media outlets as a vocal proponent of justice for all victims of clergy sexual abuse. Based on his handling of a situation with Father Paul Freemont, pastor at St. Edward Catholic Church in Springfield, it appears that the bishop needs a lesson in practicing what he preaches.

The Catholic Church across the United States has been under fire for some time with allegations of widespread cover-ups involving clergy and the sexual abuse of minors. Robertson has been quoted numerous times as saying that these cover-ups are inexcusable and would never be tolerated in his diocese. He has pledged total transparency in the Diocese of Fairview. There now seems to be some question of what and what does not constitute transparency in the eyes of Bishop Robertson.

Earlier this year, Robertson removed Father Paul Freemont from his role as pastor of St. Edward after several individuals had accused Freemont of sexual assault. The alleged assaults occurred over twenty-five years ago at St. Joseph Seminary in Rutherford County. Freemont was principal of St. Joseph from 1968 until it closed its doors in 1978. Six former students and one former teacher, all but one of whom wishes to remain anonymous, have reported that they approached Robertson earlier this year with allegations of abuse by Freemont in the 1970s. The most serious of those allegations comes from Ryan Williams, who claims he was assaulted by Freemont repeatedly over a four-year period when he attended high school at St. Joseph.

None of the other allegations involve physical abuse, but rather sexual comments and innuendoes made to students by Freemont at the all-male high school. Bishop Robertson, who will retire in a few months, conducted an internal diocesan investigation, and recently returned Freemont to active ministry at St. Edward after a six-week, forced leave of absence. This investigation, as well as the decision to return Freemont to his position as pastor, appears to have been handled by Robertson alone. While the Diocese of Fairview does have an official panel in place whose job it is to investigate allegations of abuse made against clergy, Robertson apparently failed to notify the panel members of the situation, instead choosing to oversee his own investigation.

During those six weeks when Freemont was on leave, devoted parishioners remained unwavering in their support of the popular pastor. There were weekly prayer vigils held at St. Edward to support Freemont. It is rumored that a group of parishioners even started a fundraising campaign to help with what will certainly be daunting legal bills. Freemont has denied any impropriety, but the former students and their coach say otherwise. Apparently, Bishop Robertson's superior, Cardinal Keith Santana, is not happy with Robertson's handling of the investigation. Santana has forced Robertson to report Freemont to the Rutherford County authorities. While no criminal charges have yet been filed, sources at the Rutherford County district attorney's office indicate that charges will likely be forthcoming once the sheriff's investigation is complete.

The diocesan investigative panel, made up of laypersons, also appears to be unhappy with Robertson's unilateral handling of the accusations against Freemont. As of this report, four of the six panel members have resigned, citing frustration with being denied the right to investigate the charges against Freemont.

In the meantime, Freemont remains as pastor of St. Edward Catholic Church. Phone messages left for Freemont and his attorney have not been returned.

CHAPTER SIXTEEN

THE CHARGES

So then, now that we have been justified by faith, we are at peace with God through our Lord Jesus Christ; it is through him, by faith, that we have been admitted into God›s favour in which we are living, and look forward exultantly to God's glory.

Not only that; let us exult, too, in our hardships, understanding that hardship develops perseverance, and perseverance develops a tested character, something that gives us hope, and a hope which will not let us down, because the love of God has been poured into our hearts by the Holy Spirit which has been given to us.

~ Romans 5:1-5

Once that article was published in the *Daily Times,* all hell broke loose. There were camera crews from every local television news station within a three-hour drive of Fairview camped out in the church parking lot all day. The phones in the parish office rang non-stop. Newspaper reporters from all over the state called asking for quotes. Parishioners called and stopped by the church, wanting to know what was happening and offering to help if they could. Other parishioners called to say that they wouldn't set foot inside of St. Edward as long as I was still pastor, or that they'd never donate another dime to the church as long as I was there. We were a church divided.

Adeline was working eighteen hours a day. We had to keep the doors to the church building locked all day, something we had never done. If someone wanted to come in to pray or to come to the parish office, they needed to call first, then someone on staff or a volunteer would meet them at the door to let them in. The building felt more like a crypt than a place of worship, and the parking lot looked like a circus. The few days that I went to the church, I stayed in my office with the door closed, and when I left, it was through the back door. I canceled all of my appointments—no counseling, no marriage-preparation, no committee meetings. Most days, I didn't even leave home. What was the use? My being on site was a distraction for everyone. As hard as it was to be accused of abuse, it was even harder to see St. Edward turned upside down like that.

This went on for just over two weeks. The whole time I waited for the phone call from Bob James, the call where he would tell me that Rutherford County wasn't pressing charges, that it was all finished, and that my life could start getting back to normal. Waiting for that call, knowing that it would all be okay, was what got me through those weeks. It was the last Monday of August, a week before Labor Day, when the call finally came.

"Paul, it's Bob. I called the parish office. Adeline said you hadn't been in for a few days. Are you okay?"

"I'm fine. It's just easier to stay at the house. I can't be there right now, it's too hard. Please tell me you're calling to tell me this is over."

"I'm sorry, Paul, I really am. I just got off the phone with the district attorney's office. They've decided to press charges. The good thing is that I was able to convince them not to send the sheriff to arrest you. I offered to drive you in on Wednesday instead. I'll pick you up at the house. Then we'll drive to the sheriff's office in Rutherford. When we get there, they'll explain the charges to you, fingerprint you, take your picture, then you'll be released on personal recognizance, and I'll drive you back home. Believe it or not, it works a lot like you see on television."

"They're arresting me? For what? I didn't do anything wrong! I can't believe you're even saying this. This is a nightmare!"

"They're charging you with felony sexual assault against a minor and misdemeanor simple assault. Three counts of felony assault, Williams, Simon, and Dodson, and two counts of misdemeanor simple assault, Michaels and Davis."

I interrupted Bob to point out the obvious. "Michaels and Davis admitted that I did not *touch* them. How in the world am I being charged with assaulting them?"

"That's the tricky part. Michaels and Davis said they felt *threatened* by you, so technically the D.A. can charge you with misdemeanor simple assault. Unlike battery, assault doesn't require physical contact. If the alleged victim is in *fear* of being injured, then they can make a charge for simple assault. I know it sounds ridiculous. It's such a gray area, in my opinion. Unfortunately, that's the law, and it's not up to us. The D.A. gets to make that call. After you're released on Wednesday, we'll sit down and start making a plan for how to proceed going forward. Next Tuesday, you'll go before the judge for your arraignment. That's a week from tomorrow. We have a lot to do in the next eight days. Try not to worry too much. We'll get through this. I'll pick you up Wednesday morning at nine o'clock."

And that was it. In forty-eight hours, I would be arrested. And in the meantime, all I could do was wait.

My waiting was interrupted the next day when I went to the mailbox and saw a copy of the *Virginia Catholic* waiting for me. On the front page, above the fold, was a letter from Bishop Robertson. His retirement was coming up, and this would be one of his last official statements to his faithful flock.

The letter was appropriately titled, *Forever Trust in the Lord, For the Truth Shall Reign.*

As I write this to you all, the faithful of the Diocese of Fairview, I do so with much gratitude. I have served as your bishop for nearly two decades, and during those years I have been overwhelmed by the goodness and generosity that you have shown in your daily lives. You are truly people of Christ, and as people of Christ, much is expected of all of us. We are called to practice love, acceptance, and forgiveness. But we are also called to be just and fair and to protect those who cannot protect themselves.

As you all know, the Catholic Church has been under much scrutiny in recent years due to the uncovering of clergy abuse that goes back decades. Our diocese has not gone untouched by this, and I have always promised you that I would do everything in my power to prevent this reprehensible behavior, to punish those who are guilty of it, and to provide needed resources to victims.

Accusations of abuse must be investigated thoroughly, but they must be investigated properly as well. The unfortunate incident years ago with Father Jeffrey Stevens showed us how important it is that investigations into such delicate matters be handled following very precise processes and procedures. That is why I chose to personally oversee the diocesan investigation into allegations of sexual misconduct made against Father Paul Freemont, pastor of St. Edward Catholic Church in Springfield, when they were initially brought to my attention. At the onset, there was one accuser. I conducted a thorough investigation, including extensive psychological testing of Father Freemont, and concluded that the accusation could not be substantiated. I saw no reason to investigate further, nor to have the Diocesan Clergy Investigative Panel conduct any additional investigation. According to the terms of the Dallas Charter issued by Rome, I was under no obligation to have the panel investigate. I stand by that decision as the appropriate one, given the circumstances I was aware of at that time. There has been criticism lodged against me for my handling of this situation with Father Freemont, and this criticism is unfair. I have handled this situation to the best of my ability as your bishop, given the information provided to me at the time.

However, several more individuals have come forward in recent months and have made a variety of accusations against Father Freemont, dating back several decades to his time as principal of the now closed St. Joseph Seminary in Rutherford County. With these new allegations come additional concern, and I must remain true to my promise as bishop that I will always seek justice for those who have been wronged by any member of the clergy in this diocese. For that reason, I have chosen to notify the Rutherford County sheriff's department and have asked them to conduct their own investigation into the happenings at St. Joseph during Father Freemont's tenure there. This was a very difficult decision and one I made after much time spent in contemplation and prayer.

Father Freemont will remain as pastor of St. Edward during the course of the sheriff's investigation. As my time as your bishop nears its end, I assure you that my successor, whomever that may be, will make the appropriate decisions regarding Father Freemont's continued service to the Diocese of Fairview.

Yours in Christ,
Bishop Thomas Robertson

That son of a bitch! Robertson's letter made it sound like I was guilty, but he made sure he covered his ass.

CHAPTER SEVENTEEN

THE ARREST

Blessed is anyone who perseveres when trials come.
Such a person is of proven worth and will win the prize of life,
the crown that the Lord has promised to those who love him.

Never, when you are being put to the test, say,
'God is tempting me'; God cannot be tempted by evil,
and he does not put anybody to the test.

~ JAMES 1:12-13

Bob arrived to pick me up at nine o'clock sharp on Wednesday morning. The forty-five-minute drive to the Rutherford County courthouse went by like it was five minutes, but I guess that's how it goes when you're terrified of what you're getting ready to walk into.

Once again, I was sweating so much that it was seeping through my clothes. I had to continually remind myself to stop twisting my ring.

Between the weight loss from not eating and the nervous sweating, my ring had loosened to the point that I thought it might hit the floorboard of the car.

We arrived a few minutes early for the ten o'clock appointment. How unusual to have an appointment to be charged with sexual assault and arrested, but Bob was right—this way was better than having a sheriff arrive at the house, or even worse, come to the church office and take me away in handcuffs.

The entire process took less than an hour. The deputy who read me my rights was pleasant, even jovial. He didn't seem to judge me, instead acting like we were long-lost friends who had just reconnected. He looked vaguely familiar, and I wondered if he'd ever been to Mass at St. Edward. After I indicated that yes, I understood the charges, and I was aware of my rights, I was fingerprinted and photographed. Then I was told it was okay to leave.

"See, I wasn't lying, was I? Almost exactly like you see on television. How about if we get an early lunch and start working on a plan?" Bob was trying so hard to lighten the mood—as if that were even possible.

"There's a diner a few miles from here off of Route 240. I'm guessing it's still open," I replied. "When I was at St. Joseph, we used to go there when we needed a break. Sneak off for a cheeseburger and a beer." Suddenly it hit me, riding down those back roads in Rutherford, talking about the time at St. Joseph. This was really happening. They had arrested me for sexually assaulting a student—no, students—and I may very well go to jail.

We arrived at the diner, parked, and went inside. It looked absolutely the same, like something out of the 1950s. Red-and-white striped leather on the silver-trimmed booths, red-speckled Formica tabletops. I remembered the first time I went there, the night we all met with the psychiatrist who was going to help us figure out how to turn the struggling school around.

Bob found a large booth toward the back with plenty of room to spread out. He opened his notebook to start working on our strategy for the following Tuesday. We had six days.

I excused myself and went straight to the men's room. Luckily it was empty, so I found a stall with a door, locked myself in, and cried like a baby. I'm not sure how long I was in there; it seemed like forever. Bob must have sensed that I needed some time, because he didn't say a word when I got back to the table. There was a club sandwich and a glass of Diet Coke waiting for me when I sat down. I'm sure my face was a sight, but Bob never mentioned it.

"Okay," he said, "let's get working on a plan."

We pulled into the parking lot at the courthouse for the arraignment the next Tuesday morning, bright and early—me, Bob, and Adeline. I'm not sure what I expected, but what I saw absolutely shocked me. Standing on the courthouse steps were at least 200 parishioners from St. Edward, some crying, some praying the Rosary.

As I walked up the steps with Bob and Adeline on either side of me, they met me with hugs and pats on the back.

"We're all praying for you, Father."

"Oh, Father, we know you're innocent."

"Father, God knows the truth. Everything will be fine."
      Bob and I walked inside and took our seats. Adeline sat behind us. The judge walked out just a moment after, with the normal formality by the bailiff to *all rise*.

As soon as we sat down, the bailiff called my case.

"Case 2824126, Rutherford County versus Paul E. Freemont. Mr. Freemont, please come forward." I hadn't been addressed as *Mister* since

1965. I had been *Father or Reverend* for over forty years, but this certainly wasn't the time to correct the bailiff on the proper way to address a Catholic priest.

Bob reached over and gave me a nudge. I couldn't move. "Paul, walk up there."

I had seen my psychiatrist a few weeks ago, and he'd given me a prescription for anxiety. He told me to start taking it right away, to give my body time to adjust. I had put off taking it until that morning, but now I could see that had been a bad idea. I felt like I couldn't think. Everything felt fuzzy.

When I approached the bailiff, he said, "Please state your full name."

"Paul Edgar Freemont." I managed to get that much out.

He handed me a Bible. "Mr. Freemont, do you swear that the information you shall give to the court in this matter shall be the truth, the whole truth, and nothing but the truth, so help you God?"

"Yes, I do." So far, I was okay.

"Please take your seat."

The judge studied the papers in front of him, frowning as if he didn't like what he saw. I was certain that small-town judges have a special hatred for people accused of sexually abusing minors.

"Reverend Freemont, is this your attorney sitting with you?"

"Yes, Your Honor."

"Reverend Freemont, you have been charged with three counts of felony sexual assault, and two counts of misdemeanor simple assault. Do you understand those charges?"

As much as I wanted to proclaim my innocence, I knew that I had to stick to the plan that Bob and I had made. "Yes, Your Honor."

"Reverend Freemont, I see that you were read your rights when you were taken into custody. Do you understand those rights?"

"Yes, Your Honor."

"Reverend Freemont, I see that you have chosen to waive your right to a jury trial, and that you are prepared to enter a plea at this proceeding. Is this correct?"

I glanced at Bob, who nodded. "Yes, Your Honor."

"Reverend Freemont, are you guilty of the three counts of felony assault that you have been charged with?"

"No, Your Honor, I am not guilty." It felt surprisingly powerful to say it out loud to a judge.

"Reverend Freemont, are you guilty of the two counts of misdemeanor assault that you have been charged with?"

"Your Honor, I'd like to plead no contest to those charges."

Bob and I had spent the last six days debating this part of the plea. To me, it felt like an admission of guilt. Bob disagreed, and ultimately, he convinced me to make the plea. He had continually reminded me that there were no guarantees, whether I chose a jury trial or waived that right and allowed the judge to decide my fate. Bob also pointed out the harsh reality that my vocation as a Catholic priest was almost certain to work against me.

I had naively assumed that justice would prevail regardless of the widespread anti-Catholic sentiment that intensified every time another priest was accused, which was, unfortunately, a frequent occurrence. As painful as it was to think that I could be found guilty simply because I was a Catholic priest, I finally agreed with Bob that making a plea of no contest was the best thing to do.

"Reverend Freemont, do you have any questions for this court?"

"No, Your Honor."

"Then this court is adjourned until three months from today, Wednesday, December tenth. On that day, I will render my decision regarding sentencing. Reverend Freemont, you will remain free on your own recognizance until that time. You may not leave the state."

The bailiff stepped in. "All rise." The judge left the courtroom, and that part was over.

CHAPTER EIGHTEEN

THE SILVER LINING

My child, if you aspire to serve the Lord, prepare yourself for an ordeal. Be sincere of heart, be steadfast, and do not be alarmed when disaster comes. Cling to him and do not leave him, so that you may be honored at the end of your days. Whatever happens to you, accept it, and in the uncertainties of your humble state, be patient, since gold is tested in the fire, and the chosen in the furnace of humiliation.

~ Sirach 2:1-5

I kept a very low profile for the next three months. I went to the church only when I had to, and the only appointments I made were ones that couldn't be avoided. That wasn't hard, actually, because people were clearly avoiding me. Attendance at Mass had dropped by about thirty percent—the collection basket even more.

I presided over the five liturgies every weekend, but I left through the back door as soon as I could. I had Lewis Waller, the retired priest, and the deacons handle the baptisms and weddings that were already on the calendar. No one seemed to mind when Adeline called to tell them that Father Waller or one of the deacons would be taking my place as the celebrant.

The silver lining was that I knew, deep down, this would fade with time. People would someday look at me without suspicion, without wondering if it were all true. Holding onto that thought was what made the days bearable. There were still times when I wondered if I could go on, if perhaps St. Edward would be better off without me. Looking out into pews that were only partially full, knowing there had been standing room only at just about every liturgy until a few months ago, was so hard. And to look up during liturgy and see a stranger, head down, taking notes, knowing it was another reporter—that was even harder.

I was eager for December tenth, sentencing day, to arrive. Bob had assured me there was virtually no chance I would serve any jail time. My plan was to rebuild my life starting on December tenth. I could begin to heal, move forward, and put all of this behind me. It would be a day of rebirth for me.

By the time the sentencing day arrived, I was suffering from full-blown anxiety. My psychiatrist had me on a cocktail of anti-depressant medication, which numbed the pain just enough to allow me to continue to function and get through the day. I was eating only enough to keep me going.

The crowd at the courthouse was twice as big as it had been three months ago when I came for the arraignment. I recognized some, others I didn't. I could hear them praying as I approached the steps to go inside, my hand holding tight onto Adeline's arm as we walked up the stairs, Bob on the other side of me.

Bob had been very specific about what I was to wear and how I was to act. The judge had presumably made his decision before we arrived for sentencing, but Bob reminded me that you can't be too careful. I wasn't to wear anything that made me look like a Catholic priest. I needed to look as normal as possible, as if the judge might forget who I was and why I was there.

It was finally the day that the *before* ended and the *after* began. That's how my life would be defined going forward: *before* and *after*. But this would all be over, and I would begin to heal. My parish would begin to heal, and that was the actual silver lining.

Once we were seated, the bailiff went through the courtroom formalities. I thought of what Bob had said so many months ago; it really was almost the same as depicted on television.

"Reverend Freemont," began the judge, "on the three charges of felony assault, I find you not guilty. Since you pled no contest to the simple aggravated assault charges at your arraignment in this courtroom in September, I have no choice but to sentence you according to the guidelines of the state of Virginia associated with that plea. Therefore, I am sentencing you to a two-year jail term on the two counts of misdemeanor simple assault, with the entire two years suspended. I am also ordering that you remain on probation for the remainder of your life."

It was over. *After* was here.

The next day I was sitting in my parish office, feeling as if I might actually begin to rebuild a normal life, when the intercom buzzed on my office phone. Adeline's voice came through. "Father, Bishop Robertson is on the line. He says it's urgent."

The last thing I wanted that morning was to be trapped in a conversation with Robertson. I was certain he'd be filled with false congratulations, telling me that truth and justice had prevailed. He would surely tell me he never doubted my innocence, and he'd likely invite me out for a drink to celebrate. There was no way I would accept that invitation after he reported me to the sheriff and wrote that article in the *Virginia Catholic* where he all but called me guilty. Besides, he was a few weeks away from retirement, so it would be easy to avoid him.

"Bishop, good morning. It's good to hear from you."

"Paul, I'm so sorry. I got a fax not five minutes ago from Cardinal Santana. I can't do anything about this. Trust me, I would if I could. And even if I could, it would only be temporary. I'm retiring in less than three weeks. They haven't chosen a bishop to take my place yet, so Santana will be in charge during the interim."

"Bishop, what are you talking about?" I wondered if he had already had a drink that morning.

"The fax, Paul. The cardinal says that you need to be out. Today. You need to leave St. Edward. You're not the pastor anymore, and you can't live at the rectory anymore. In fact, you can't live anywhere within the boundaries of any parish where you've ever served. He's giving you twenty-four hours."

I sat in shock before mumbling something along the lines of *I understand* before hanging up the phone and asking Adeline to come into my office and sit with me. Then I called Bob. His secretary put me through right away, and he promised to get to the bottom of it. I left the office and went back to the rectory, wondering if I should start to pack. I asked Adeline to go with me. The thought of being alone was more than I could stand.

Bob called an hour later. "This seems to be legitimate. I just spoke with the diocesan attorney. Santana has been put in charge of the Fairview diocese since the bishop is retiring this month without a replacement. I spoke with someone in his office. The diocese owns the rectory, so if they say you can't live there, then you can't. And Santana is your boss, in the eyes of the Church, and in a few weeks, he'll be the acting interim bishop of the diocese. If he says you're not pastor, then you're not. He can do this, and it looks like he has. I wish I had a different answer. You should pack. You need to clean out your office and be moved out of the rectory by five o'clock tomorrow. I bought you a few extra hours. Santana has someone coming at five tomorrow to change the locks at the house. You're not allowed to perform any duties as clergy, anywhere."

This was unreal. Robertson knew about the Alford Plea. We had discussed it, and he had encouraged it. He had agreed with me that it was in the best interest of the parish, and of the diocese, to end this as quickly as possible. There had been no mention of my leaving St. Edward or of moving out of the rectory.

"Paul? Paul? Are you there? Did you hear me?"

"Yes."

"Do you need me to send someone to help you? Will you go to your townhouse?"

"No. Thank you. Adeline is here. I'll call my brothers and a few other people who will want to help. And, yes, I'll go to the townhouse."

I had bought a little townhouse a few years ago, about fifteen minutes away from St. Edward, and fortunately, it was within the boundaries of a different parish. It was in a quiet neighborhood, very peaceful. I had used part of the money my parents left me as a down payment and spent the last few years fixing it up, little by little. It was my refuge, my escape. I'd go there to be alone sometimes. Most of my parishioners didn't even know I had it. My plan had been to move there when I retired, which I had thought was years away.

My brothers arrived with boxes and borrowed pickup trucks, and a few close friends came to help pack. They moved me out before midnight. Adeline had gone back to the church to pack my office so the rest of us could focus on the rectory. I rarely spent the night at the townhouse; I usually just went there for the day. Between the strange environment and the questions burning inside of me, my first night there was rough.

I couldn't understand how all of this had happened, and how it had happened so quickly. I made a plea of *no contest* to a misdemeanor charge, not a felony, because my attorney thought that was the easiest way. There had been no felony conviction.

Bob had said there was no doubt in his mind that if we ended up going to trial, we would win, but my name would be mud by the time it was all over. The media had not been kind to me during the whole ordeal. We had no idea I was going to be removed from St. Edward. Now, less than twenty-four hours later, the cardinal changed everything.

I was in total shell shock.

PART THREE

PURGATORY

─────────◉─────────

When the Son of Man comes in his glory,
and all the angels with him, then he will sit on his glorious throne.
Before him will be gathered all the nations,
and he will separate them one from another
as a shepherd separates the sheep from the goats.

~ MATTHEW 25:31-32

─────────◉─────────

CHAPTER NINETEEN

YESTERDAY IS GONE

Blessed are those who are persecuted in the cause of uprightness:
the kingdom of Heaven is theirs.

Blessed are you when people abuse you and persecute you and
speak all kinds of calumny against you falsely on my account.

Rejoice and be glad, for your reward will be great in Heaven;
this is how they persecuted the prophets before you.

You are salt for the earth. But if salt loses its taste,
what can make it salty again? It is good for nothing
and can only be thrown out to be trampled under people's feet.

~ Matthew 5:10-13

I settled into a routine pretty quickly, all things considered. I had been a priest for thirty-eight years, and then—just like that—I wasn't. The thing that drove me crazy was wondering why it happened the way it did.

Bishop Robertson had known about the Alford Plea for three months before my sentencing. He encouraged me to do it, saying he agreed that it was the best choice. Then, less than twenty-four hours after I left the courthouse, he got a fax from Cardinal Santana telling him I had to leave. Knowing how slow the Catholic Church is to act on anything, this didn't make sense. Someone must have called Santana and told him about the sentencing. I suspected it was Bishop Walters, but I could never prove it. And, the reality was, it didn't matter.

The first few months were an adjustment, but fortunately, I had Adeline and a group of devoted parishioners from St. Edward to help me find my way. It was time to figure out how to live my life as someone other than a parish priest.

Having the townhouse was a blessing. At least I had a place to live, but there were bills to pay. The legal bills had taken quite a toll on me financially. My diocesan salary of forty thousand a year only went so far. A group of parishioners from St. Edward and St. Francis Xavier had come together months ago to raise money for my legal fees, and that had covered a big chunk. The balance was being paid monthly. My budget was tight, and the balance in my savings account was rapidly going down. I had thirty thousand dollars left in savings. My attorney had warned me that my legal bills could be well over two hundred and fifty thousand dollars by the time it was all over. And I wasn't sure it was over.

Starting a new life at sixty-four seemed overwhelming. The worst part was not knowing what to expect as time passed. I didn't know what would happen to my salary or my pension. Technically, I was supposed to work until age seventy, and then I'd receive a pension from the diocese for life.

Now I wondered if I'd ever see my retirement from the diocese. As unbelievable as it sounds, I was in total limbo, as far as the diocese was concerned. I wasn't assigned to a parish, and I wasn't allowed to perform any of the duties of a priest, yet they had not stripped me of my faculties. I continued to receive my paycheck from the diocese, and I was still covered by their health insurance. I didn't know what the rules were for this type of situation. I was terrified to ask any questions because I didn't want to draw attention to myself. I was apparently out-of-sight and out-of-mind as far as the diocese was concerned, and it was probably best to keep it that way.

I rarely left my townhouse in the beginning. Adeline did my grocery shopping, and that was really all I needed. A small group of friends would come to visit, although there were many more who sent notes or called on the phone to check on me. Most of the phone calls went to voicemail; it was too hard to talk about the same thing over and over.

Sometimes people showed up at the door unannounced; I made sure to keep the blinds closed so that I could pretend no one was home when they knocked. After I knew they were gone, I'd open the door, sometimes to find that they'd left something for me, like a loaf of homemade bread or even a coconut pie, which those closest to me knew was my favorite.

Behind the closed blinds, I would often sit in my recliner watching movies on the VCR. I loved going to the movie theater, but I couldn't risk going out in public and running into someone who knew me, so rental tapes picked up by Adeline were the next best thing.

You can watch movies all day for only so long before it gets old, even for a movie buff like me. It was time to focus on my new life—and on how to make a living. I needed a career change. It was time to come up with a way to use what I knew, and that was religion. I also wanted to do something that I could be passionate about. That's when I came up with the idea for a class called *Religion in Film*.

I told one of my friends, Lynne, about that idea, and a few days later, she and I were sitting at the computer ordering VHS tapes of my ten favorite movies. I spent months studying those movies and developing an outline for the class that I dreamed of someday teaching. That kept me busy, and eventually there were days when I wasn't consumed with mourning my past life.

It was almost as if Santana had forgotten about me as soon as he removed me. I was just happy that I seemed to be off of the radar as far as the Church was concerned. That all changed a year later when a new bishop was appointed to serve the Diocese of Fairview.

Bishop Samuel Benedetto was the polar opposite of Robertson—rigid, harsh, dictatorial. Benedetto, interestingly, had never served as a *pastor* of a parish, yet somehow, he had managed to move up the ranks to become a bishop. His duties as a priest had always been administrative, and he had spent the past twenty years of his career living in a tropical paradise thousands of miles away.

The question on everyone's mind was this—what had he done to be kicked out of paradise and sent to Fairview, Virginia? Whatever he did, it must have been big. I can say, based on the way he handled my situation, that he was one of the most unpastoral people I've ever encountered in my life.

A week after they appointed Benedetto bishop of the Fairview diocese, I received a letter from him in the mail. He assured me that I had not been forgotten, and that bringing me to *true justice* was one of his top priorities in his quest to fix the Diocese of Fairview. I wasn't quite sure at the time what he meant by *fix*, but I learned the answer to that later.

Apparently, Benedetto's opinion of Robertson's tenure as bishop was that the inmates had run the asylum. His intention was to rule Fairview with an iron fist, and to be certain that every employee in the diocese, priests included, knew that he was in charge, that he made the rules, and that he expected nothing less than complete obedience.

I should have expected something like this, but I had buried my head in the sand, hoping it would never happen. I called Bob and read the letter to him, and we waited to see what was next.

CHAPTER TWENTY

IN THE DARK

And they, all locked in the same sleep, while that darkness lasted—
which was in fact quite powerless and had issued from the depths of
equally powerless Hades—were now chased by monstrous specters,
now paralyzed by the fainting of their souls; for a sudden,
unexpected terror had attacked them.

And thus, whoever it might be that fell there stayed
clamped to the spot in this prison without bars.

Whether he was ploughman or shepherd, or somebody at work
in the desert, he was still overtaken and suffered the inevitable fate,
for all had been bound by the one same chain of darkness.

The soughing of the wind, the tuneful noise of birds
in the spreading branches, the measured beat of water in its
powerful course, the headlong din of rocks cascading down,
the unseen course of bounding animals, the roaring of the most
savage of wild beasts, the echo rebounding from the clefts
in the mountains, all held them paralyzed with fear.

~ WISDOM 17:14-19

What happened next was nothing, at least for three months. Bob had called the chancery the day after I received the letter from Bishop Benedetto. Bob requested a meeting with him, but the bishop declined. His secretary (someone new since Norma had retired along with Bishop Robertson) informed Bob that he would be contacted if the bishop chose to meet with him or me in the future.

Once again, there was nothing I could do but wait. The bishop was holding all the cards, and it terrified me.

I had been filling my time for the past few months working on the *Religion in Film* curriculum, which I hoped would come to fruition one day as a real college class. I had developed what I thought was a pretty good outline for it, and I decided to see what I could do to make it a reality.

Adeline suggested I reach out to one of the parishioners from St. Francis Xavier, who was a department head at Central Virginia Community College. We spoke on the phone, and he seemed to like the idea, so he connected me with the head of the Social Science department.

Within a week, I had a meeting to discuss my new venture as an adjunct professor at CVCC. The meeting went well, although the outcome wasn't quite what I expected. CVCC wasn't ready to commit to the *Religion in Film* class, but they needed someone to teach an Ethics 101 class in the evenings, which met twice a week. This was mid-December, and the class was scheduled to start in mid-January. The professor who was scheduled to teach the class had become very ill, and they needed a quick replacement, or they would have to cancel the class.

We came up with a compromise. I would start out at CVCC by teaching the ethics class with a one-semester commitment. If that went well, then we'd continue for the second semester. After that, we would discuss putting the *Religion in Film* class on the roster and see what interest it generated.

In the interest of full disclosure, I made sure that CVCC was aware of my situation—that I had been arrested for assault, had pleaded no contest, and was on probation for life. My biggest fear was that it would end my new career before it even got started. Surprisingly, the administrative staff at CVCC wasn't concerned. Apparently, the department head was aware of all of it before meeting with me and had already had a discussion with the human resource department. They saw no legal reason to deny me the position. I officially had a new career as a college '*prof.*'

The new semester was just four weeks away when I accepted the job, so I had a lot to do to prepare to start teaching. I had never taught a college class before, but it was exciting to have something to look forward to. And I needed to generate some income. Adeline was a tremendous help with getting me prepared to teach. Even though she was still working at St. Edward, she'd come to the townhouse every night after work to help me get organized.

When classes started, Adeline went with me to every one of them, two evenings each week. We joked with the students that she was my administrative assistant, and they all seemed to love having her in class.

Midway through the semester, I received a second letter from Bishop Benedetto. This one was to inform me that he had petitioned Rome to look into my case and had requested that they laicize me. I knew what it meant to be laicized; I would still *technically* be a priest but could no longer preside at liturgy or administer any of the sacraments. I'd already been told that I couldn't do any of that, so I wasn't sure what he hoped to accomplish at that point. What I really wanted to know was how that would impact me financially. Would the paychecks from the diocese keep coming? Would I receive retirement benefits?

I turned things over to Bob, and he said that he would meet with the bishop to see exactly what all of this meant. Just like the first time when he called the chancery to make an appointment to see Benedetto months before, the bishop's secretary turned him down again. This time, though, she took his contact information and said that someone from the chancery would be in touch.

A week later, a third letter from Bishop Benedetto arrived in the mail, and this time, they sent a copy to Bob's office. The letter instructed me that all future communication initiated by me or Bob be directed to the diocesan attorney. It also suggested that I retain the services of a canon lawyer.

The following day, Bob reached out to the diocesan attorney, who was, fortunately, willing to take his call. Unfortunately, he was absolutely no help at all. He told Bob that he knew nothing about my current situation. The bishop had *turned it over to Rome* (whatever that meant). He suggested that we follow the instructions in the latest letter and hire a canon lawyer to assist.

A canon lawyer is a licensed attorney who specializes in the legal system of the Catholic Church (known as canon law). Most canon lawyers attend seminary before law school, so they know the teachings and workings of the Church inside and out. Since neither Bob nor I had any idea what was going on with Benedetto, we decided that my hiring a canon lawyer was the next logical step. The closest lawyer I could find was in New York, and he couldn't see me for four months.

CHAPTER TWENTY-ONE

NEW SET OF RULES

Thus, condemnation will never come to those
who are in Christ Jesus,
because the law of the Spirit which gives life
in Christ Jesus has set you free from the law of sin and death.

What the Law could not do because of the weakness
of human nature, God did, sending his own Son
in the same human nature as any sinner to be a sacrifice for sin,
and condemning sin in that human nature.

~ ROMANS 8:1-3

The four months waiting to meet with Richard Morris, the canon lawyer, flew by quickly because of my teaching schedule.

The student reviews from the first semester were pretty good, and CVCC asked me to come back for a second semester and teach two sessions of Ethics 101. I would teach one class that met two evenings a week, and one class that met once a week at night. It was a win-win for me. Teaching two classes of the same subject meant one subject to prepare for and twice the income. By this time, it was summer 2005, eighteen months since they had removed me as pastor of St. Edward. While the pain was still very real, it wasn't as sharp as it had been.

My meeting with Richard was set for early July, a Tuesday, at two o'clock in the afternoon. This was right between the spring and fall semesters, so the timing was perfect. I spent the early part of the summer gathering everything I could think of that might help him sort this out: notes from the meetings with Bishop Robertson, copies of newspaper articles, transcripts of the arraignment and sentencing, the letters from Bishop Benedetto. I sent Richard a box filled with all of this information two weeks before our meeting.

Bob and I made the nine-hour drive north to New York State the day before our meeting with Richard. It would have been much cheaper to fly up and back the same day since I was paying Bob by the hour, but I've always been terrified of airplanes. Plus, I had waited four months for this, and I wasn't going to take a chance going up the day of the meeting. Bob indulged me and drove me up, even though it meant spending two nights in a hotel.

Richard had told us that he expected our meeting to last three to four hours, minimum. Since we were coming such a long distance, he had agreed to clear his calendar for the afternoon so that we could get as much done as possible in one meeting.

Between Bob's three hundred dollar an hour fee and Richard's five hundred and fifty, plus the cost of two hotel rooms for two nights, this was going to be an expensive meeting. I didn't want to repeat it more often than was absolutely necessary. I was grateful more than ever for the income from my teaching job, even though it paid barely enough to cover my new legal expenses.

Richard's high-rise office was even more impressive than Bob's, with the distinctive smell of wealth greeting us as we stepped off of the elevator, its expansive city view, and expensive furniture.

Richard was much younger than I expected, probably not even forty yet. He was very easygoing, laid-back, and casual, but he certainly knew canon law. He had read over everything I sent him, so he was very familiar with the situation by the time we all sat down in his office. Richard promised me that we would be finished in time for dinner, albeit a late one.

We spent the next five hours listening to Richard explain how I had gotten to this point.

"Paul, are you familiar with the *Congregation for the Doctrine of the Faith?* Maybe you've heard it called the CDF? It's a book of canon law put in place by Pope John Paul II in 2001. It basically states that, as of April 2001, the Church authorities at the Vatican, Rome, have complete authority over issues involving Catholic clergy who are involved in any type of sex abuse accusation. Until 2001, the bishop of each diocese was allowed to deal with these cases as he saw fit. The bishop could then decide whether or not to have the Vatican investigate, depending on the outcome of the bishop's own investigation."

"Richard, I'm not sure I understand what that means for me. This all started in 1997. It went on until 2003, and I never heard anything about the Vatican becoming involved. If this all changed in 2001, then why am I just hearing about this now?"

"Well, it appears that you may have fallen through the cracks, so to speak. Bishop Robertson was, technically, handling things according to canon law. *In the beginning, that is.* For whatever reason, he followed the doctrine of canon law only up to a point when Ryan Williams made his second accusation in early 2002."

"Up to *what* point?" I asked, probably a little more abruptly than I should have. Richard was simply trying to explain all of this to me, but I didn't like what I was hearing.

"Robertson was following procedure when he investigated the accusations the second and third times, in 2002 and again in 2003. Canon law still left the preliminary investigation to be handled by the bishop at the diocesan level. Where he messed up was that he stopped too soon. The CDF requires the bishop to make a report to the Vatican *every time* a member of the Catholic clergy is investigated for accusations of sexual abuse, unless the accusations are proven false *beyond a doubt*. If there is any chance that the accusations could be true, then the bishop must request that the Vatican investigate. That's where Robertson messed up." Richard's explanation was annoying me. Was he on my side or not?

"It sounds to me like Bishop Robertson handled it the right way, because I was innocent. I am innocent." I hoped that Richard could understand that there was no way the accusations against me had been true.

Richard shook his head. "Paul, I get where you're coming from. I really do. But I've read everything you sent me, plus I've done some research on my own. Even you have to admit that this wasn't a cut-and-dry case of false accusations."

"So, you don't believe me? You think I'm guilty?" I wondered if we should end the meeting and move on. But I wasn't sure what the next move would be if Richard couldn't help me.

Bob chimed in at that point. "I don't think that's what he's saying."

"Then what *is* he saying?" I said, perhaps a little louder than I should have.

"I'm sorry," Richard said, "you've totally misunderstood my point. Let's set the record straight. I do not think you're guilty. But this isn't up to me. Right now, it's up to the Vatican. According to the CDF, Bishop Robertson should have asked the Vatican to open an investigation in 2002 when Ryan Williams came back around. At that point, it was your word against his, and there was no way to determine, beyond a doubt, that you were innocent. Then in 2003 when you took the Alford Plea . . ."

"Yes, I took the Alford Plea because I wasn't guilty." Richard was an attorney. Surely, he could understand that.

"You took the Alford Plea because you knew there was evidence that a judge or jury *could* use to find you guilty. You knew then that it looked bad and there were no guarantees if you went to trial. This was another point when Robertson should have turned things over to the Vatican."

So, that was it. Benedetto did what Robertson hadn't, and he was actually playing by the rules.

"What now?" I was sure I didn't want to hear the answer, but I had to ask.

"Now, we wait. I'll reach out to the Vatican, but I don't have high hopes of getting a quick response. If I had to guess, I'd say this could take years. I'll bill you monthly for my time, but I don't think it will be much since we'll do more waiting than anything. Luckily, you're not on anyone's radar except Benedetto's. I suggest keeping a low profile, don't do anything to rock the boat or draw attention to yourself."

I wasn't sure what that meant, but I'd heard it before.

CHAPTER TWENTY-TWO

YEARS OF WAITING

While at table with them, he had told them not to
leave Jerusalem, but to wait there for what the Father had promised.
'It is,' he had said, 'what you have heard me speak about:

John baptized with water but, not many days from now,
you are going to be baptized with the Holy Spirit.'

Now having met together, they asked him,
'Lord, has the time come for you to restore the kingdom to Israel?'

He replied, 'It is not for you to know times or dates that the Father
has decided by his own authority, but you will receive the power of
the Holy Spirit which will come on you, and then you will be my
witnesses not only in Jerusalem but throughout
Judaea and Samaria, and indeed to earth's remotest end.'

~ ACTS OF THE APOSTLES 1:4-8

Richard was right; we waited for years. He had reached out to the CDF officials at the Vatican right after our meeting in 2005. He received a letter in response, months later, letting him know they had received my file and they would open an investigation at some point. They gave no timeline and no guidance as to how we were to proceed going forward.

Richard and I touched base every six months or so, and every time he told me the same thing. "No news is good news, Paul. We just need to play this waiting game."

There were days when I actually managed to forget that my life was a live grenade, and the Vatican had its hand on the pin.

Teaching classes at CVCC is what kept me sane during the months and then years of waiting to hear what, if anything, the Vatican would do about my case. My Ethics 101 classes became very popular and were always full with a waitlist. I would even have a former St. Edward parishioner sign up for my class once in a while, and Adeline and I always loved that. She had become as much a fixture in my classes as I had. The students always seemed to enjoy having her there in class, and I certainly loved having her there with me. Although she and I were almost exactly the same age, some of the students thought she was my mother! We had a lot of fun with that.

The *Religion in Film* class finally came to fruition in my second year at CVCC, but it wasn't as popular as Ethics, so they offered it every other semester. The classes weren't usually full, but enrollment was always high enough to keep them from being canceled. Still, it was my favorite class to teach.

The other things that kept my sanity in check were visiting with former parishioners and presiding over Mass every day. Daily Mass had been part of my life since I was a seven-year-old altar boy almost six decades ago, and I couldn't imagine a day without it. Those that I was closest to knew that about me and often asked if they could join me for my private celebration of liturgy. Being placed between the proverbial rock and a hard place, I couldn't say no, but I couldn't say yes. According to Bishop Benedetto, I was allowed no *public* sacramental celebration, but what kind of priest says no when someone requests to join you in celebrating Mass? I found myself explaining, many times, that I was required to celebrate Mass alone, and that I would be doing so at precisely this time on this day. If my doorbell rang five minutes before my celebration was to begin, then I had no choice but to welcome the visitor into my home. I also reasoned that if I presided over liturgy in my living room, then technically, it wasn't *public.*

I had been told by both Bishop Robertson and my canon lawyer to keep a low profile, not to do anything that would draw attention to myself. I had made it my mission to stay under the diocesan radar. So many times over those *waiting* years people asked me to perform weddings and baptisms, but I had to say *no.* It was awful, turning down people who had been so faithful and devoted to me. I just couldn't take a chance by celebrating a sacrament in a public setting. I knew that if I gave Benedetto any reason to make my life harder, then he would. I was receiving my diocesan pension, but it terrified me that one day those checks would stop coming. I had no idea how I could survive if that happened.

I never met Bishop Benedetto in person, but he continued to disrupt my life for years. Every time I began to feel like something close to normal, Benedetto would pop up again. Every few months I'd get a letter from him, as if he needed to be sure I knew that I wasn't forgotten. In his letters, he'd remind me that I was still under investigation by the Vatican, and until that investigation was complete, I remained a priest who couldn't function as a priest. I could not perform any duties as clergy, and I could not participate publicly in any sacrament. I was allowed to say Mass as a priest. They expected me to say Mass, but I had to do so alone.

As hard as it is to admit, I lived my life in fear. I'd always focused on the *what if,* but now I was consumed by it.

What if the Vatican never made a decision? What would happen to me? How could I live the rest of my life without an end to this? But if they made a decision, what would that be? What would happen then?

What if I ran out of money? How would I pay my bills? How much longer could I teach? Could Benedetto simply stop the diocese from paying my pension? What would I do if he did? How would I afford to pay more legal fees?

What if the people who had stood by me decided one day that I wasn't worth it, and they abandoned me? Could I survive being alone?

What if I went to my grave without ever proving to the world that I was an innocent man?

EPILOGUE

They have been saying all our plans are empty.
They have been saying 'Where is their God now?'
Roll away the stone, see the Glory of God.
Roll away the stone.

__Freemont, Father Paul E.__, departed this life suddenly on August 4, 2016. He was preceded in death by his brothers, Marvin Freemont and Lucas Freemont, and his parents, Andrew and Julia Freemont. Father Freemont is survived by several nieces and nephews. His memory will be cherished by many, especially his devoted friend, Adeline Jennings. A private burial took place on Thursday, August 11, 2016, at All Souls Cemetery in Fairview. Father Freemont was ordained in 1965 by Bishop Theodore Saunders. Father Freemont received his undergraduate degree in philosophy from St. Bartholomew College and his graduate degree in theology from St. Michael College. He also received a master's degree in secondary education from St. Agnes University. Father Freemont was the founding pastor of three parishes: The Catholic Church of the Resurrection in Mooresville, St. Francis Xavier Catholic Church in Fairview, and St. Edward Catholic Church in Springfield. He served as a priest for the Catholic Diocese of Fairview for 50 years. Father Freemont had a talent for drama and homiletics. His greatest love, until the day of his death, was the Catholic Church. He will be missed by many.

A LAST MESSAGE FROM LYNNE STRAHORN

Father Paul Freemont's case filled St. Edward with controversy. The parish was divided into three camps. There were those who were certain he was guilty, those who were unwavering in their support of his innocence, and those who didn't want to hear about it anymore, hoping it would all just go away if they turned a blind eye. St. Edward lost a number of parishioners, ironically, from both of the first two camps. There were those who left because of his presumed guilt; they couldn't bear to attend a parish connected to such horrific accusations. Others left because they were convinced of his innocence and never got over the pain of losing their favorite priest under such unimaginable circumstances. They couldn't bear to walk through the door at St. Edward, knowing that he would never be back.

Father Paul (and Adeline) continued to teach ethics and religion class-es at Central Virginia Community College for eight years. He was one of their most popular teachers, with classes usually filling up on the first day of registration. This was always a point of great pride for him, and he thrived in his second career as a college professor—a *prof,* as he liked to be called.

On the fortieth anniversary of his ordination to the priesthood, two years after he was removed as pastor of St. Edward, Father Paul celebrat-ed by having dinner with a small group of friends at his favorite Italian restaurant, a little family-owned place just a few minutes down the road from St. Edward. On his forty-fifth anniversary and again on his fiftieth, he chose to commemorate the occasion privately.

A few years after his death, a small group of parishioners at St. Ed-ward, a handful of people who had never met Father Paul, petitioned Bishop Benedetto to have St. Edward remove all signs of Father Paul from the building and grounds. Benedetto was happy to accommodate. Father Paul's portrait on the wall as Founding Pastor, the plaque on the multi-purpose room indicating *Freemont Hall,* and the stone bench in the courtyard purchased by parishioners in honor of his dedication to the parish were all removed quietly and without rebuttal.

Adeline eventually retired from St. Edward, but she remained active in the parish as long as her health allowed. A devout Catholic her entire life, she believed in acceptance, forgiveness, and the profound grace of God. Her support of Father Paul never wavered. She was his most de-voted friend until his death, almost thirteen years after he was removed from St. Edward.

Father Paul and I visited regularly after he left St. Edward. Some-times we would go for long walks, one of the things he loved to do. Other times we would sit in the living room of his townhouse, eat-ing a sandwich or a piece of coconut pie and reminiscing about our mutual friends.

Our conversations were always harmless, with lots of catching up on *who's doing what,* although he liked to joke that we were getting together to *name names and trash reputations.* He always laughed when he said that, as if our meetings were filled with mischief. In reality, we'd spend our hours talking about those we both loved and sharing our own personal challenges.

Looking back, I realize I did much more talking than he did. He never shared a confidence belonging to anyone else, ever. I remember many times when his phone rang while we were together. He'd check the caller ID, and he'd answer if it was Adeline because he knew she was calling to check on him; she'd worry if he didn't answer. He'd answer the phone and tell her he was with *someone* and would call her back later. He never disclosed who he was with, no matter who it was. Your privacy was carefully guarded when you were with him.

At one of our lunch meetings several years before his death, Father Paul asked me for a favor. He wanted me to tell his story.

He and I spent hours together in the following months as he shared the details of his life, some of which he said he had shared with no one before. That was fifteen years ago, and now I have finally gathered the courage to tell his story. At his request, I have fictionalized many details of his story to protect the privacy of those involved: the names of people and places, dates, and other identifying information.

He had some very specific ideas on how to proceed once *Unholy Scandal* was published. One, I would present it as *based on a true story*. Two, we needed to try to get the book chosen by Oprah's Book Club; he was a big fan. And three, if the story were made into a movie, Tommy Lee Jones would play the role of Father Paul (Father thought he looked like Tommy Lee Jones).

Father Paul died without resolution. The Vatican never completed the investigation into the accusations made against him, and no one was ever completely certain that an investigation was ever started by the Vatican.

Lynne

PART FOUR

THE BACKGROUND

In the beginning God created heaven and earth.

Now the earth was a formless void, there was darkness over the deep,
with a divine wind sweeping over the waters.

God said, 'Let there be light,' and there was light.

God saw that light was good, and God divided light from darkness.

~ GENESIS 1:1-4

The Catholic Church has been a controversial institution since its inception by Jesus Christ in the first century. The Church—with its sacraments and saints, its rituals and rites—continues to be enveloped in an aura of mystery that tends to both confuse and mesmerize Catholics as well as non-Catholics to this day. The Church is often seen as radical and extreme. There are those who call the Church a cult, and there are those who deny that Catholics are actually Christian. One thing is certain: the Catholic Church is shrouded in misunderstanding. Human nature being what it is, people often fear (and sometimes even loathe) that which they don't understand; the Catholic Church is no exception to this. The Church is an easy target for enmity and hatred, particularly by the mainstream media.

The Catholic Church has its own set of laws. In 1917, those laws were put into a single code called *Canon Law*. Canon law outlines the rules and regulations of the Catholic Church. There are 1,752 canons (laws) divided among seven books.

BOOK ONE: The basics of the code of Canon Law, the General Norms, are contained here. This book contains canons dealing with issues on the diocesan and parish levels.

BOOK TWO: The rights and obligations of clergy and laypersons are found here. The hierarchy of the Church is also outlined in Book Two.

BOOK THREE: The rules for Catholic teaching (from basic catechesis to university level) and preaching are found here.

BOOK FOUR: Sacraments are the focus here. This book covers the canons for receiving and administering the seven sacraments.

BOOK FIVE: This book is basically about Church property law. It also deals with finance, contracts, and wills.

BOOK SIX: Criminal Law is outlined here and explains the authority of the Church to punish, the crimes that are punishable, and the associated penalties.

Book Seven: Processes such as trials, procedures, court organization, rights, and appeals are found here.

Canon law does not override civil or criminal legal systems in any locality.

In 1985, a Catholic priest in Louisiana admitted to molesting eleven boys. This is often viewed as the beginning of the Catholic clergy sex abuse scandal in the United States. The real beginning of the crisis could perhaps go back as far as the year 1950, when Church leaders began to hear rumblings regarding the sexual abuse of children by Catholic clergy. We will likely never know for sure how far back in time this goes.

The Catholic Church made national headlines in the early 1990s when a number of books were published detailing allegations of sexual abuse of children, mostly boys, by Catholic clergy. The scandal intensified into the early 2000s as it became clear that many United States dioceses and their bishops had ignored or covered up innumerable allegations of sexual abuse over many years. The Church was in crisis seemingly overnight. Both the United States Catholic Church and the Vatican came under fire for their mishandling of abuse allegations dating back decades.

Catholic bishops were accused of covering up abuse allegations by moving accused priests to different parishes, allowing those priests to continue having contact with children while the parishioners were unaware. Many of these bishops, like the accused priests that they had protected, either retired or accepted a forced resignation. Millions of dollars were paid to the victims by the dioceses that were at the center of the abuse. Both the financial and social impact on the Church were daunting, prompting the United States Conference of Catholic Bishops to adopt a policy of *zero tolerance* in June 2002 with the Charter for the Protection of Children and Young People. A policy of *zero tolerance* can be a double-edged sword with its swift and severe justice for the *presumed guilty*—some of whom are *not* guilty.

A Google search for *sexual abuse of children in religious organizations* will provide millions of results (as of this writing, there were over sixty million). The majority of those search results contain the word Catholic and link to articles and/or studies involving the sex abuse crisis in the Catholic Church. Far fewer link to information about sex abuse in non-Catholic religious organizations. It would be naïve to believe that the sexual abuse of children in organized religion is a uniquely Catholic issue. However, the Catholic Church is an easy target; it's an institution that the media loves to hate.

While there is clearly a heavy focus on the crisis in the Catholic Church, a deeper search will uncover allegations and admission of child sexual abuse in innumerable other religious organizations. Baptist ministers, Episcopal priests, Lutheran pastors, Jewish rabbis, Jehovah's Witness pioneers, Mormon bishops, and Muslim imams are just a few examples of religious leaders who have made headlines for accusations of child sexual abuse in the United States.

THE HIERARCHY OF THE CATHOLIC CHURCH

The Catholic Church is a highly structured organization. There is a chain of command that helps both the Church and her followers understand the complex organization of *who, what, when, and where.* There is a hierarchy for the people as well as for the places. The Catholic Church is often referred to using feminine pronouns (*her* and *she*), as the Church is considered to be the Bride of Christ.

CATHOLIC PARISH

The parish is where Catholics attend weekly services (Mass). A Catholic priest, a pastor, leads the parish. Parishes are often named after a saint (ex: St. Mary Catholic Church) or after a term related to Jesus

Christ (ex: Catholic Church of the Redeemer). The parish is where Catholics receive the sacraments (confession, baptism, communion, marriage, etc.).

CATHOLIC DIOCESE

The diocese is a geographical region made up of a number of local parishes. In the United States Catholic Church, a state may have multiple dioceses, or the entire state may be in one diocese. For example, the state of New York has eight, but that includes one located in Hartford; Virginia has two, Richmond and Arlington. The bishop is in charge of the diocese, and every priest in the diocese reports to the bishop.

CATHOLIC ARCHDIOCESE

The archdiocese is basically a large diocese and is run by an archbishop. It is a geographical region with a large Catholic population, usually in a large city. An archdiocese is usually located in a major metropolitan area (ex: the Archdiocese of San Francisco).

THE VATICAN

The Vatican, an independent nation located in Vatican City, Rome, is at the top. The pope, the leader of the Church, rules the Church from his home at the Vatican.

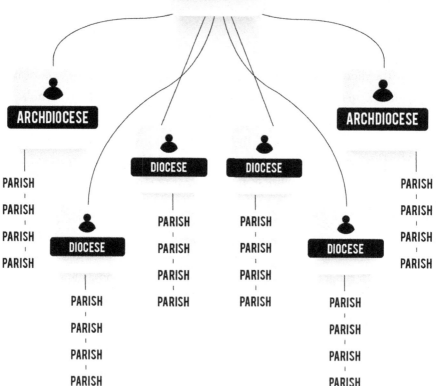

THE HIERARCHY OF THE CATHOLIC CHURCH*

The Parish is where people go to attend Mass (to worship).
A Priest/Pastor leads the Parish.

The Diocese is made up of many parishes in a geographical area.
The Bishop leads the Diocese.

The Archdiocese is a geographical area with a large population.
It is basically a large diocese typically located in a metropolitan area.
The Archbishop, sometimes a Cardinal, leads the Archdiocese.

Vatican City, an independent nation located in Rome,
is the seat of the Catholic Church.

The Pope leads the Church from his home at the Vatican.

a very basic, simplistic overview

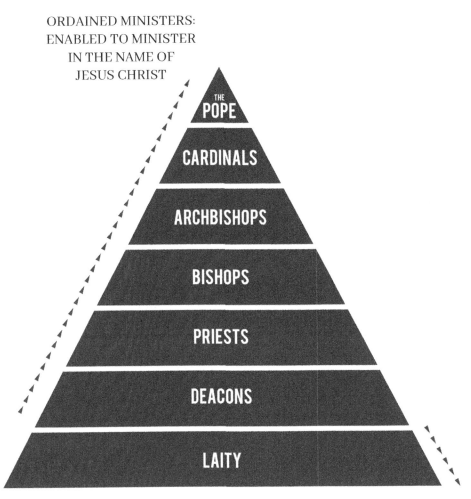

ORDAINED MINISTERS:
ENABLED TO MINISTER
IN THE NAME OF
JESUS CHRIST

THE
POPE

CARDINALS

ARCHBISHOPS

BISHOPS

PRIESTS

DEACONS

LAITY

MEMBERS
OF THE CHURCH,
NOT ORDAINED

DEFINITIONS

Absolution—the forgiveness of sin granted by a Catholic priest.

Ad Limina Visit—bishops (from a given region) travel to Rome and meet with the Pope to discuss issues that are specific to their region.

Alb—a full-length, long-sleeved tunic worn by a priest or deacon, usually white.

Archbishop—high-ranking bishop, the head of an archdiocese, may be a cardinal.

Archdiocese—a large diocese, led by an archbishop.

Baptism—the first sacrament one receives in the Catholic Church, usually as an infant. A priest or deacon immerses the candidate for baptism in water or sprinkles water on the forehead to cleanse the candidate of original sin. The parents of the child are affirming responsibility for raising their child in the Catholic faith when they have their child baptized Catholic.

Bishop—Catholic clergy, ranks above a priest, typically is in charge of a diocese.

Canon Law—the rules and regulations which govern, guide, and direct the Catholic Church.

Cardinal—nominated by the pope, advises the pope; some are *electors* who elect the new pope. As of July 2021, there were 221 cardinals worldwide.

Catechism—a set of questions designed to teach one about the Catholic Church.

Cathedral—the principal church in the diocese, run by the bishop.

Catholic—worldwide, universal.

Catholic Church–Roman Catholic Church for purposes of this book.

Chancery—the administrative office of the diocese.

Christian—a follower of Jesus Christ; Catholics are Christians.

Church—meant to refer to the Catholic Church when used alone and capitalized.

Communion—also known as Holy Communion. A sacrament in the Catholic Church which commemorates the Last Supper that Jesus had with the apostles. The bread and wine become the body and blood of Jesus Christ.

Confession—also known as penance. Disclosing your sins to a priest, hoping he may grant you absolution in the name of God.

Confirmation—a ceremony during which a Catholic receives the gifts of the Holy Spirit. Takes place typically when one is a teen or possibly adolescent. The confirmand assumes responsibility for their religious life when they are confirmed.

Consecration—making something holy. Catholics believe that the priest consecrates the bread and wine during the Mass, causing transubstantiation, meaning that the bread and wine become the body and blood of Jesus Christ.

Deacon—ordained minister in the Catholic Church. There are two types of deacons: transitional and permanent.

Diocese—made up of many parishes in a given geographical area, led by a bishop.

Eucharist—a Catholic sacrament. The priest consecrates the bread and wine, which then become the body and blood of Jesus Christ through the mystery of transubstantiation.

Faculties—the right to act on behalf of the Church, granted to priests and deacons (to perform baptisms, weddings, etc.). If a priest's faculties are taken away, he cannot act on behalf of the Catholic Church.

Genuflect—bending one knee to the ground as a sign of respect.

Holy Orders—a sacrament during which a man becomes a priest or deacon and receives faculties.

Holy See—also known as The See of Rome, The Vatican.

Holy Spirit—the third person in the Trinity (Father, Son, Holy Spirit). The spiritual presence of God in the world. There are seven gifts of the Holy Spirit: Wisdom, Understanding, Counsel, Fortitude, Knowledge, Piety, and Fear of the Lord.

Judas—one of the twelve apostles. He betrayed Jesus.

Laicize—remove faculties and return an ordained minister to status of laity.

Laity—church members, not ordained.

Liturgy—public acts of worship.

Marriage—the legal union that joins two people. A man and a woman in the Catholic Church, a sacrament.

Mass—Catholic religious service that includes the Liturgy of the Word and Eucharist.

Monsignor—honorary title that may be given to a priest.

Ordination—one of the seven sacraments; a man becomes a deacon or priest and is enabled to perform duties in the name of the Catholic Church.

Parish—a church community where worshipers gather, typically led by a priest.

Parochial—related to a parish, supported by a parish (ex: parochial school).

Permanent Deacon—an ordained minister in the Catholic Church who may be married. May perform all the duties of a priest except last rites, consecration of the precious body and blood, and absolution of sin.

Pope—the head of the Catholic Church.

Priest—ordained minister in the Catholic Church, typically the leader of a parish, but may be assigned administrative or other duties within a diocese.

Purgatory—a place or a process of purification where the souls of those who die remain as they prepare for Heaven.

Rectory—the residence of a priest.

Rome—capital of Italy and its largest city.

Sacrament—a sacred, holy rite that grants divine grace through Jesus Christ. There are seven sacraments in the Catholic Church: Baptism, Penance/Confession, Eucharist, Confirmation, Holy Orders, Marriage, Anointing of the Sick/Last Rites.

Sin—voluntarily doing something wrong that separates you from God. Sins are either mortal or venial. Mortal sins are serious (evil, immoral) acts; venial are less serious.

Transitional Deacon—a level of ordination on the journey to being ordained a priest.

Transubstantiation—changing form; the bread and wine become the body and blood of Jesus Christ when consecrated by the priest during Mass.

Vatican—home of the pope, located in Vatican City, Rome.

Vatican City—a city-state and the world's smallest country by both population and geographical size.

Vatican II—also known as The Second Vatican Council, established in 1962. The Church became more modern, more liberal.

REFERENCES

Author's Notes

Prayer for Healing Victims of Abuse. Copyright by the United States Conference of Catholic Bishops. Used with permission.

https://web.archive.org/web/20220216174518/https://www.usccb.org/prayers/prayer-healing-victims-abuse

Prayer for Priests. Pope Benedict XVI, written for the Solemnity of the Sacred Heart, July 1, 2011.

https://web.archive.org/web/20220216174614/https://zenit.org/2011/06/23/benedict-xvi-pens-prayer-for-world-rosary-relay/

Acknowledgements

Yesterday is Gone. Saint Teresa of Calcutta.

https://web.archive.org/web/20220216174702/https://en.wikipedia.org/wiki/Mother_Teresa

Preface

Ringo Starr, English musician, singer, and songwriter

Introduction

The Alford Plea.

https://web.archive.org/web/20220216183901/https://en.wikipedia.org/wiki/Alford_plea

Xanax. Medication used to treat anxiety disorders.

https://web.archive.org/web/20220216174851/https://en.wikipedia.org/wiki/Alprazolam

Assault, Virginia Law.

https://web.archive.org/web/20220216174936/https://www.findlaw.com/state/virginia-law/virginia-assault-and-bat-%20tery-laws.html

PART ONE AND THROUGHOUT

Bible Verses, New American Bible. No permission required.

https://web.archive.org/web/20220216175009/https://www.usccb.org/offices/new-american-bible/permissions

Chapter Three

Pontiac Bonneville is an automobile built by Pontiac from 1957 to 2005. Pontiac is a registered trademark of General Motors ®

Chapter Five

Child's Play. Robert Marasco.

https://web.archive.org/web/20220216175050/https://playbill.com/production/childs-play-royale-theatre-vault-0000010220

PART TWO

Never Give Up. Message to Generation X from Pope John Paul II.

https://web.archive.org/web/20220216175720/https://www.catholicmom.com/articles/2014/05/07/what-st-john-paul-the-great-had-to-say-to-generation-x

Chapter Eleven

Diet Coke® is a trademark of the COCA COLA COMPANY®

PART THREE

Chapter Twenty-Two

Congregation for the Doctrine of the Faith, defends Catholic Doctrine

https://web.archive.org/web/20220216175856/https://en.wikipedia.org/wiki/Congregation_for_the_Doctrine_of_the_Faith

Epilogue

Roll Away the Stone © 1993, Tom Conry. Published by OCP. All rights reserved. Used with permission.

Oprah's Book Club ®. The Oprah Winfrey Show book discussion club.

https://web.archive.org/web/20220216180028/https://en.wikipedia.org/wiki/Oprah%E2%80%99s_Book_Club

Tommy Lee Jones. American actor and film director.

https://web.archive.org/web/20220216180121/https://en.wikipedia.org/wiki/Tommy_Lee_Jones

PART FOUR

The Background

GOOGLE ® is a trademark of GOOGLE INC.

Sex Abuse of Children in Religious Organizations. Reference websites:

https://web.archive.org/web/20220216180310/https://www.usccb.org/upload/FAQs-canonical-process-sexual-abuse.pdf

https://web.archive.org/web/20220216180337/https://www.simplycatholic.com/introduction-to-canon-law/

https://web.archive.org/web/20220216180918/https://en.wikipedia.org/wiki/Catholic_Church_sex_abuse_cases_in_the_United_States

https://web.archive.org/web/20220216181153/https://childusa.org/wp-content/uploads/2020/10/Archdiocesan_Policies_WhitePaper_10-1-20s.pdf

https://web.archive.org/web/20220216181346/https://www.usccb.org/offices/child-and-youth-protection/charter-protection-children-and-young-people

https://web.archive.org/web/20220216181606/https://en.wikipedia.org/wiki/Sexual_abuse_cases_in_Southern_Baptist_churches

https://web.archive.org/web/20220216181731/https://www.episcopalnewsservice.org/2021/03/12/pittsburgh-bishop-receives-complaint-of-child-sexual-abuse-against-former-priest/

https://web.archive.org/web/20220216181807/https://www.timesofisrael.com/questions-over-alleged-coverup-of-sex-abuse-claims-against-us-reform-rabbi

https://web.archive.org/web/20220216181928/https://www.timesreporter.com/story/news/2021/04/30/steven-p-woyen-resigned-lutheran-pastor-when-allegations-surfaced/7411396002/

https://web.archive.org/web/20220216182026/https://www.dailyherald.com/news/20210527/trial-scheduled-for-jehovahs-witnesses-elders-accused-of-failing-to-report-sexual-abuse

https://web.archive.org/web/20220216182129/https://www.opb.org/article/2021/02/23/oregon-man-sues-mormon-church-over-alleged-sexual-abuse/

https://web.archive.org/web/20220216182302/https://www.reuters.com/world/asia-pacific/pakistani-cleric-charged-with-sexual-abuse-religious-school-2021-06-17/

https://web.archive.org/web/20220216180310/https://www.usccb.org/upload/FAQs-canonical-process-sexual-abuse.pdf

https://web.archive.org/web/20220216182506/https://subscribe.buffalonews.com/e/limit-reached-bn?returnURL=https://buffalonews.com/news/local/does-catholic-church-have-bigger-sex-abuse-probem-than-other-religions/article_e3fe40a8-7af7-59cd-b060-3ea8b95210da.html

https://web.archive.org/web/20220216182711/https://www.law.georgetown.edu/gender-journal/wp-content/uploads/sites/20/2020/01/Article-4.pdf

https://web.archive.org/web/20220216175856/https://en.wikipedia.org/wiki/Congregation_for_the_Doctrine_of_the_Faith

Definitions

https://web.archive.org/web/20220216182926/https://www.dummies.com/article/body-mind-spirit/religion-spirituality/christianity/catholicism/the-hierarchy-of-the-catholic-church-192934

The Hierarchy of the Catholic Church

https://web.archive.org/web/20220216183051/https://en.wikipedia.org/wiki/List_of_Catholic_dioceses_in_the_United_States

https://web.archive.org/web/20220216183539/https://en.wikipedia.org/wiki/Roman_Catholic_Archdiocese_of_New_York

https://web.archive.org/web/20220216183717/https://www.usccb.org/beliefs-and-teachings/vocations/priesthood/priestly-formation/faqs-priesthood-ordination-seminary

Made in the USA
Middletown, DE
21 August 2022

71932557R00106